Metaphorosis

October 2021

Beautifully made speculative fiction

Also from Metaphorosis

<u>Verdage</u>

Reading 5X5 x2: Duets
Score – an SFF symphony
Reading 5X5: Readers' Edition
Reading 5X5: Writers' Edition

<u>Metaphorosis Magazine</u>

Metaphorosis: Best of 20xx
Metaphorosis 20xx: The Complete Stories
annual issues, from 2016

Monthly issues

<u>Plant Based Press</u>

Best Vegan Science Fiction & Fantasy
annual issues, from 2016

from B. Morris Allen:
Susurrus
Allenthology: Volume I
Tocsin: and other stories
Start with Stones: collected stories
Metaphorosis: a collection of stories

Metaphorosis

October 2021

edited by
B. Morris Allen

ISSN: 2573-136X (online)
ISBN: 978-1-64076-209-1 (e-book)
ISBN: 978-1-64076-210-7 (paperback)

Metaphorosis

a magazine of speculative fiction

from
Metaphorosis Publishing

Neskowin

October 2021

Ennui Tea

Ivy Grimes

Estella, the seemingly ageless proprietor of Dour Power Café, hired me the day I slumped in. I ordered a small cup of Ennui Tea (which honestly tasted like vinegar), quietly thrilled to have a new goth cave to hide in. Nowhere else in town was safe from patriotism, town pride, and school spirit.

I didn't even ask for the job. She seemed to know I needed one.

The only question she asked in my job interview was: "Are you happy?"

"Only fools are happy," I said.

"Well…no, but that's a start," she said as she tossed me my apron.

She told me right away that she was an herbologist, a witch who made potions, and that she went from town to town helping people ditch their false performance of joy and embark on the rocky path to enlightenment.

"Like some nonconsensual Oprah?" I asked. Estella seemed more like a hippie than a witch, and I could tell she'd let me get away with some impertinence.

"They only drink if their spirit is willing. I give them what they're searching for, even if they don't know they're searching."

It sounded ridiculous.

"I *believe* you, though," I said. "Why do I believe you?"

"I'm very persuasive when you want to believe," she said.

Of course, she was right. For once I actually wanted to trust someone, though I hated to admit it. She was the strangest person I'd ever met, and I wanted to be just like her.

I started the job that very afternoon, expecting all the cheery, pastel-clad people I'd gone to high school with to walk in, wrinkle their noses at the stark interior, and walk right out again. Instead, Estella's magic made the place as attractive to them as a Target Starbucks, and she made them fans of bitter drinks like Ennui Tea and Doldrums Coffee. Within a week, both the chatty churchgoing types and the arrogant preppy types were wearing tight black jeans and reading poetry.

Like any good goth, I'd always dreamed of being a witch myself. Estella kept telling me she saw something special in me—some spark of power in my honesty. She kept inviting me to attempt her spells, but I declined. She said failure was part of the process, but I didn't want to fail in front of the only person I'd ever met who seemed to think I was special.

Most days, I worked out front alone while she performed her magic rituals in her private office, but sometimes she'd come out and unsuccessfully try to sell people more advanced drinks, little nudges along the path to enlightenment. Estella had spent most of her long life in places like Berlin and Paris and New York, and ours was the first Midwestern town where she'd set up shop. She thought that in a small town, it would be easier to see the difference she was making. I tried to explain the Midwest to her, but she just didn't understand the crushing burden of forced niceness and optimism. Melancholy was such a relief for my fellow townspeople that they weren't willing to exchange it for more heavy-lifting. People had been telling them to smile their whole lives, and they were finally having a rest from insincerity. Stuff like self-actualization seemed way too taxing to them.

After a couple of months of fruitless salesmanship, Estella was discouraged. One rainy Monday, she stood beside me at the front counter and looked out at our bleak clientele and asked, "Why don't our customers *want* to become enlightened, Eris? Why do they only order Ennui Tea and Doldrums Coffee? Why won't they try the Self-Acceptance Cold Brew, or even a simple Epiphany Tea? I've sold my potions in dozens of different towns, and I've never encountered a group so stubborn and stagnant."

"Well..." I didn't want to remind her I hadn't tried her more advanced drinks yet either. "I keep telling you—I'm not sure they can handle any more. It's a miracle they've come this far."

"Melancholy is only the first stage of enlightenment, Eris. Despair at the awful plight of the world is supposed to inspire us to grow and help others grow. I know you're capable if you open your mind. But please do it quickly! I need your help to appeal to your fellow townspeople."

Her advice would have annoyed me even more if she hadn't already told me I was the most mature person in town. Although based on how she described the other people in town, it didn't seem like much of a competition.

"Are *you* enlightened?" I asked her with as much politeness as I could manage.

"I'm on my way. That's why I'm here, to help others along the path."

So even she wasn't entirely enlightened. At least she was honest with me.

"I don't understand why it has to be so serious," I said. "Why can't this just be a cool place to hang out?"

"Do you find this place cool?" she said, gesturing at the clientele.

I liked the way everyone had changed. No one was propping up the world like Atlas anymore—no more catchphrases, no more masks of joy, no more pretending. On the other hand, I could see why Estella might find her new customers dull. Now they all acted like they had the flu, and they could only talk about mortality.

"They need to find the satisfaction in sadness." I loved heartbreaking songs and movies where everyone died in the end, and I took pride in drifting around town like a shadow. Most people thought I was miserable, but it took talent to find the perverse joy I'd found in misery. Due to Estella's powerfully depressing concoctions (sold with panache by yours truly), I was finally on-trend.

Estella shook her head at me and smiled the way that people in their 30s (or in Estella's case, her 130s) smile at people in their early 20s. I hated it when she treated me like I was a child wearing a paper crown.

"Someday you'll taste a melancholy fruit so bitter, it will open your eyes. Then you'll want to help others through their suffering," she said. Or prophesied.

I didn't have to wait long for the prophecy to be fulfilled. The next day, I fell in love.

A guy walked in wearing grandpa slacks and a baggy button-down shirt and thick glasses and an addictive smirk. He was charming and sensitive, witty and intense. He said his name was Berlin, and he went to college a few towns over and had been looking everywhere for a cool place to hang out.

He teased me about my stereotypical goth look—heavy makeup and funereal garb. But he said it was cool I'd named myself Eris, after the Greek goddess of conflict and being pissed-off. I teased him about carrying a copy of Sartre's *No Exit* under his arm like a first-year philosophy major.

"I *am* a first-year philosophy major. I'll be a sophomore this fall," he said.

"I'm not going to college. It's a waste of time," I said.

He shrugged. "It's only a waste of time if you aren't becoming enlightened."

There was that word again. To me, enlightenment was a product sold on TV, like an acne medication that promised more than it could deliver. But it made people feel good, as if salvation were just around the corner.

"College is too expensive."

"It all depends on your perspective. But yes, I won't relish paying back my student loans with my philosopher's salary." He smirked again, and I rolled my eyes, but I was already obsessed with him.

He asked what I recommended from the menu, and I poured him a cup of

Doldrums Coffee (pre-magicked by Estella), but it didn't seem to dampen his high spirits. He had the enthusiasm of a kid on Halloween, and we were running the haunted house.

Estella came out from her office and asked him what he thought about Sartre. He stared at her like she was a sculpture. He'd been able to talk to me so easily, but he couldn't string two words together for her. As I watched them, my stomach began to burn. I hated Estella.

She invited him to her office where he could calm down and communicate. While they were gone, I was even more unfriendly to the customers than usual. I had never seen her take such an interest in anyone but me.

When he returned with an apron, I wasn't surprised.

"She offered me a job! And I didn't even apply! She says she sees something in me. Something special."

"Congratulations," I said without looking at him.

"And can you believe?" He got close to my ear and whispered. "She's a witch? And she can teach us some of her spells?"

"Yeah," I said, trying to pretend his breath in my ear hadn't made me shiver.

"I tried her potion, too. What can I say? She hooked me."

I found myself jealous both ways—of his regard for her and hers for him. What made him so special to her?

In spite of the awful turn of events, I still wanted to be with him, so I tried to steer the conversation to things he liked to do, to make it easy for him to invite me on a date. He kept changing the subject, asking me what I knew about magic. I tried to tell him that magic was probably painful and difficult, but he wasn't listening.

"I'm going to ask her for instructions every chance I get," he said, ignoring my cynicism. He seemed to lose interest in me for the rest of the day, which pained me more than anything. I wished we could have met somewhere else, without all the distractions. Then again, he might have looked right through me without the intrigue of my job.

It galled me when people ignored me. I'd been the town sourpuss for years before Estella arrived. People hadn't even treated me like I was weird. They'd treated me like I wasn't there. Even now that Estella had changed everything, no one credited me with being melancholy before it was cool.

For the rest of the afternoon, I listened to Berlin's charming banter as he worked the cash register. I kept my back to him, pouring drinks. The job was the best thing that had ever happened to me, but I was thinking about running away—leaving the shop and leaving town, even though realistically, I hadn't saved up enough money to move out of my parents' house.

That evening, when Estella came out to help us close, Berlin begged her for some magical secrets. He explained at length why he could be trusted, gesturing with urgency. His arms looked like the elegant tusks of some beautiful wild beast, and I wanted to know what it felt like to hold them in my hands.

"I like your enthusiasm, but you seem to think it's so simple," Estella said. She gave him the same look she always gave me—that 'what a cute kid' look. That, at least, was some relief. She clearly wasn't going to fall in love with him. He acted injured, but he said he'd ask again after work every day. And he said he was going on a thirst strike—he wasn't drinking another of her potions until she showed him how to make them. I would have fired him for insubordination, but Estella seemed to admire his intensity.

Her obvious lack of romantic interest in him made me less despairingly angry. I was able to come back to work the next day. And the day after. And the day after. All week, I worked with Berlin, and I observed not only his sex appeal, but his kindness. If I was the employee who provided the dour credibility, he was the one who cared.

By the end of the week, she finally agreed to teach him one spell—as long as I agreed to learn it with him. I wanted to resist, but one look into his eyes made me relent.

"I'll teach you how to brew Epiphany Tea," she said. She opened one of the cabinets under the counter and pulled out some of her creepy-looking materials— sticks and herbs and seeds and other dried, misshapen things.

"You don't lock this up?" Berlin asked her.

"The ingredients are inert without the magic. Magic is like enlightenment, you see," she said, giving me a serious look. "It comes upon you after hard experiences and reflection. I asked you both to work here because I can tell you've already put in some effort. You're nowhere close to enlightenment, of course, but you're on the path. After you've had a try, I'll make an Epiphany Tea for you so you can have the genuine experience."

Berlin bent his head near mine, and we stared at the instructions together.

Mix a spoonful of grated ginger with three whole cloves and a pinch of lemongrass. Boil water. As the tea steeps, think of your own past epiphanies and put your hands around the mug to imbue the drink with your energy. After five minutes, strain and serve.

"Cool, sounds easy," he said, which made Estella laugh a little. He seemed happy to have made her laugh, even though she was clearly laughing at his ignorance.

After we'd mixed up the brew, Berlin put his hands around the mug first, and without looking up at him, I put mine above his so that our hands were barely touching. It almost burned to graze his skin, but I tried to concentrate on things I'd learned in my short, pointless life. I started small, remembering when I realized I had to pedal faster to learn to ride a bike. I tried to think neutral thoughts, but of course, my mind took me to more hurtful realizations. I remembered being the only kid in the class not invited to any birthday parties in the fourth grade, realizing I was going to be alone for the rest of my life if I couldn't find a way out. I remembered the day in sixth grade when everyone partnered up to kick the soccer ball in PE, and I was left with "Stinky Sarah" again (a new girl who ate cabbage rolls for lunch and was even more unpopular than I was), and I got so mad that I hid in the bathroom for the rest of the class in protest. I'd blocked the memory. I'd forgotten that I was an asshole, too.

I looked up and saw a tear on Berlin's left cheek. What sad scenes had passed through his mind?

After several minutes, Estella told us we could stop. I stared into the pretty golden drink, and for once, I was thirsty for it. It looked so sweet, I hoped it would relieve some of the sadness I'd unearthed.

"Go ahead!" Estella said. "We can all drink. I doubt there's enough magic here to give us epiphanies, but we wouldn't want the tea to go to waste."

We each took a sip, and I waited for the earth to quake under my feet or the sky to fall to pieces overhead. Although nothing loud or sudden happened, it occurred to me that in spite of my morose attitude, I preferred to keep my life unexamined. The truth was, I'd been alone and overlooked for most of my childhood, and learning how to embrace a style of sadness had freed me. It had meant I didn't have to take things so seriously. I didn't want the fun to end by looking too closely at myself or my life.

Was that it? Was my epiphany that I'd been avoiding epiphanies?

I looked at Berlin and Estella to see if they'd learned anything. Berlin stared out the window at the waning evening light. I wanted to ask him if he was okay, but I didn't want to seem too mushy. Estella was always inscrutable to me, but even she seemed a bit shaken.

"I didn't think you'd be able to do it yet," she said. "You're both wiser than I realized. I didn't realize…"

Without elaborating, she left us. She practically ran from the front counter to her office and shut the door.

"That was weird," I said. As always, my instinct was to play it cool, but I was dying to know what Berlin's epiphany had been, so I asked him. "I don't want to be nosy, but I saw you were crying a little.

What did you realize when you drank the tea?"

He looked utterly forlorn. "I'm embarrassed to admit it."

The result of my epiphany was that I wanted to try harder to be honest, even though I hated to look like I was trying too hard at anything. "Look, you can tell me. I'll tell you first if you want."

"Okay, you go first," he said, refusing to look at me.

"I realized that…I've been a poser. I've wanted to seem deep, but I thought most of my deep thoughts when I was thirteen and depressed and alone. Things have gotten better since then, especially since I got this job, and so I haven't wanted to think about anything difficult at all. For show, I named myself after the goddess of conflict, but the truth is, I avoid every kind of discomfort. That means I'm not so different from the people I've always looked down on. Like the people who are our customers now."

My voice sounded different than usual as I made this admission. It seemed higher and squeakier, like the voice of a child.

"God. I relate so much," Berlin said. He finally looked up, and I could see the florescent overhead lights shining in his brown velvet eyes. "After I took that sip, I realized that I'm full of shit. I pretend like I'm a philosopher, but I don't know anything." He reached under the counter to pick up the book he'd brought in with him. "*No Exit.* I've been walking around with this under my arm for months to impress everyone, and I haven't read a word of it." He slammed it down on the counter.

I tried to hide my smile. I wasn't surprised.

He shrank back. "And I'm so transparent! People aren't impressed by me. They just feel sorry for me."

"Actually..." I hesitated. I wanted to take the plunge and tell him the truth, though. If I didn't take risks, how would I gain anything? "To tell you the truth, Berlin...I'm impressed by you. I think you're smart and interesting and weird and funny and...I know I just met you, but I think I really like you."

I closed my eyes so I wouldn't have to see his reaction. In the silence that followed, I hid my face in my hands.

"Forget I said anything," I said. But I didn't want him to forget.

"Look Eris, I think you're great, but I don't feel—"

"I don't want to hear it. Since you're in love with our ancient boss, why don't you stay and lock up with her? And while you're at it, tell her I quit."

With those bitter words, I took off. I went home and ignored my parents' greetings (though they didn't find that unusual), and I turned off the lights in my bedroom and listened to the saddest unrequited love songs I knew. I'd never been able to relate to them before. I'd had crushes, but I'd never admitted to having one, so it had never seemed real before. The next morning, I woke up sadder but wiser. I'd been humiliated, but it hadn't killed me. And in the process, I'd used real magic. I felt an urge to tell Estella about my heartbreak. Not only was she my witch mentor, but she was kind of my best friend.

I went into work as usual that morning. The doors were unlocked, but no one was out front. I checked the back office and found Estella peering over her notecards.

"Maybe you can find a recipe for happiness or something," I said.

"Epiphanies suck, just like I knew they would."

She gave me such a tragic, apologetic look that I felt a little guilty for complaining.

"Oh, Eris. I'm so sorry. I didn't realize how condescending I'd been to you. I hired you because I believed in you, but I kept thinking you needed to learn so much more from me before you could do anything. Like I was the key. I open certain people's eyes to magic, yes, but then I act as if I'm so much more important than they are. I rarely even bother tasting the potions my students make. But I learned something from you yesterday."

"I learned something, too. I ate a piece of melancholy fruit, just as you predicted. I fell in love-at-first-sight with Berlin and confessed it to him. And he rejected me."

"I'm sorry, Eris. Well, he quit."

"He quit?"

"He said he needed to do some soul-searching and didn't have time for a job yet. I told him to come back in a few months when he was ready."

"Did he tell you that I tried to quit?"

"No! I had no idea you were unhappy here."

"I'm not, I'm not. But I knew Berlin was in love with you and not me, and I got angry. I'm sorry I was so rash. I realized that getting my heart broken isn't the end of the world. It sucks, but it's an experience, right?"

Estella laughed. "Sure. It's happened to me seventy-three times. And I'm glad you're not quitting after all. I have more spells to teach you. But I do think Berlin will come back eventually. I have a feeling about him. Do you think it would be too hard to work with him again?"

"I'll be fine," I said, though I didn't know if that was true. I didn't know whether my feelings for Berlin were like heat lightning or a hurricane. Either way, I was curious.

"Maybe the clients need a little boost themselves," she said. "I haven't been as good at promoting Epiphany and other healing drinks as I have been at selling Ennui and Doldrums. It's my own fault. I must seem so strange to everyone since I'm not from around here. You're a much better salesperson."

"I can try talking to them. Who knows?" I said.

I went to the counter and opened Estella's secret stash and started brewing up golden cups of Epiphany Tea infused with my own fresh melancholy memories. When Kaitlyn, a former homecoming queen and recently-converted goth, walked in, I knew she was the influencer I needed. She was still the town trendsetter, and if I could convert her, I could convert them all. I told her I'd discovered the best new drink, Epiphany Tea, and I was surprised to find that she actually cared what I thought and ordered one. When she took her first sip, my heart ached for her as her face bloomed with painful recognition. I told her it was going to be all right—that everyone was full of shit, and sooner or later, we were all doomed to realize it.

That week, most of our customers starting trying Epiphany Tea after seeing Kaitlyn drink it, and ours became a more complicated café. They began showing off a range of insights and emotions, and I had to admit, I was proud of them. I stopped being rude by default when anyone walked in the door. I at least waited to see if they did anything warranting my rudeness. Making Epiphany Tea was taxing and painful at times, but when I saw how much it helped everyone, I felt like I could handle the unpleasantness.

When Berlin came back to work that December, his eyes were still velvet, but my crush had died. I was almost disappointed.

Before I showed him some of the new recipes I'd learned, I asked, "Did you ever read *No Exit*?"

"Yes," he said. "It's where that famous quote comes from—*Hell is other people.* But it turns out that he doesn't just mean that other people suck. He means it's hell to have to spend every moment impressing other people. I get it now."

I looked at him skeptically.

"Well, that is to say, I'm figuring it out."

"Me too," I said.

See Ivy Grimes's story "Ennui Tea" online at Metaphorosis.
If you liked it, leave a comment. Authors love that!
Remember to subscribe to our e-mail updates so you'll know when new stories are posted.

About the story

I must have been feeling ennui while drinking tea, because "ennui tea" came to my mind first, and the story of a young woman learning magic at a goth coffee shop followed. I imagined how great it would be to have a goth coffee shop nearby and to live in a town where everyone mopes and reads poetry all day. Yet I could see my character Estella's point that enlightenment/growth requires stronger stuff than mere disillusionment with materialism and mundanity. Growth requires confronting who you are, strengths and weaknesses alike. Acknowledging our strengths can be as mortifying as owning our weaknesses. My pessimistic protagonist Eris has to accept that sometimes she can be a shallow jerk, but she can also do magic. Her powers might not be enough to make her crush fall in love with her, but they might have more important uses.

A question for the author

Q: What other writers inspire you?

A: I'm probably most inspired by writers who cling really stubbornly to their own vision and let themselves be weird and free...like Haruki Murakami, David Lynch, Shirley Jackson, Toni Morrison, Leonora Carrington, Ralph Ellison, and so on. I also love the creepy, moving fairy tales of Helen Oyeyemi and the tragic mysteries of Tana French and the mundane humor of Barbara Pym. For "Ennui Tea", I might have been inspired by a favorite tale of retail life, Sayaka Murata's *Convenience Store Woman*, which is about a woman who loves her work at a convenience store and rejects a traditional career or family; whoever you are, you'll love it. I'm inspired by too many writers to list, though.

About the author

Ivy Grimes is originally from Alabama and now lives in Northern Virginia with her husband and beagle. She is a friendly neurotic person who writes speculative fiction and is looking for more writer friends. She feels nostalgic about her Birmingham writing group that sometimes met at an Applebees where attendees ordered the $1 house beer.

www.ivyivyivyivy.com, @IvyGri

The Tick of the Clock

J.C. Pillard

The prince followed the sound of ticking. It was not an exact science, and he'd lost his way many times as his ear tricked him with woodpeckers and creaking branches. But he always found his way again, because while the other sounds would die away, the ticking did not.

Tick, tick, tick.

He was more exhausted than he cared to admit, eyes stinging from the effort of keeping them open. His feet dragged, ploughing into the earth as though they meant to sow seeds. His clothes were dirty and sweat-soaked. The long green scarf his mother had made him snagged on every branch, and he had to wrench it loose. He thought, bitterly, that he could simply stop freeing it when it became tangled, but he couldn't bring himself to leave it.

The forest seemed to go on forever, trees growing into obscurity in every direction. The ticking drew him deeper beneath the branches, and before he knew it, the sky itself was blotted out by the tangled canopy.

Tick, tick, tick.

As the days and nights bled together, the prince realized what a foolish thing he'd done, and the dull fury which had driven him began melting to despair, the guilt he'd been keeping at bay creeping in by inches. His fingers tangled in the chain around his neck, the one holding his father's pocket watch against his breast. The voices of the palace advisors echoed in his head.

One foolish act cannot right another. You cannot undo your mother's curse with sheer force of will.

Because that's what this was, wasn't it? His mother's edict, not a law of preservation but a curse. A curse that had trapped the prince—and everyone else in his kingdom—in time for one hundred years.

Tick, tick, tick.

His food had run out two days ago. Or was it two weeks? He wasn't sure. He couldn't remember when he'd last seen a river to fill his canteen. There were many inviting places to lay his head as he trudged on: mossy patches beneath spreading trees that looked like feather beds. But he knew that if he stopped, he would not get up again.

He really did try to keep going. He *had* to keep going. Yet, his feet grew heavier and heavier until he was lifting the entire world with each step.

Step, tick. Step, tick. Step, tick. Fall.

The prince remembered the day his mother had written her edict. It had been a strange day in many ways. Only a week since his father had died, a week of black crepe wrapped over everything, of murmured apologies and condolences, of food gone half cold before he remembered to eat it. A week of his mother staring blankly forward, as though her soul had departed with her husband's.

That morning, when the prince had finally dragged himself out of bed and gone through the motions of preparing for the day, he went down to breakfast only to find his mother was not there. He thought of leaving her alone, wherever she was. God knew all he wanted was to be left in solitude to grieve in peace. But she had been so blank and empty in the past week that worry climbed up his throat and choked him, forcing him out of the dining room to search for her. He found her in what had been his father's study. She was bent over the broad oak desk, a parchment unrolled before her. The only sounds were the scratching of her quill and the ticking of the grandfather clock against the wall.

The prince cleared his throat. "Mother. Have you eaten already?"

She barely glanced at him. "I'll come down in a moment."

"What are you doing?"

She didn't answer. The prince skirted around the desk, studying the parchment beneath her fingers.

Let it here be decreed that whatsoever kills a member of the royal family shall be forever banished from the borders of this kingdom. Any harm that befalls the royal family—

The prince sighed and stepped away, letting his mother continue her writing. His father's death had been sudden—an illness that swept through and took him in less than a week. He mourned his father's gentleness and kindness, but as the days had run on, he'd started to see that he'd lost more than one parent in his father's death. As his mother's grief began to consume her, he wondered if perhaps he'd lost them both.

It won't bring him back. The words were on his tongue, but he bit down, swallowing them, and left her to her writing. At the time, it had seemed like the right thing to do, to leave her alone to carve her grief into paper. But much had happened—or, rather, had not happened —since then, and the prince had come to reflect that perhaps if he'd said something, things would have turned out differently.

Of course, now it was too late to know.

The ticking had stopped. Or, at least, it was much, much softer. That was the first thing the prince noticed upon waking.

He opened his eyes to a pine-wood ceiling whorled with age. He breathed in, evergreens and honey filling his nose. He lay in a feather bed beside an open window that looked out onto a woodland glen. Sunlight glowed through the branches of the trees outside, and he stared at those trees in disbelief. The dense, impossible forest was gone. Had he only dreamed it?

"You're awake."

Starting, the prince turned towards the creaking voice. An old woman sat beside the bed, a stretch of knitting falling on her lap. She did not look up from it as she spoke again, her needles clacking softly.

"I wasn't sure if you were going to live. But you just kept breathing steadily. You've got a strong heart."

"Where am I?" His voice cracked from disuse, and he coughed, sending pain rocketing through his body.

The woman waited for him to finish coughing and settle back against the pillows. "My house," she said, setting her knitting aside. She picked up a worn cup from the side table. "Here. Drink."

Gratefully, the prince took it from her gnarled hand. He nearly groaned as the water hit his tongue, fresh and cool. He'd been thirsty for so long he'd forgotten what water tasted like.

As he looked down at himself, the prince gasped, sloshing water over the white cotton sheets. He wore no shirt. His scarf and pack, too, were gone, as was the watch pendant. His heart began to pound, his hands to shake. No, no, it wasn't possible, it—

"Your things are in there," the old woman said, pointing to a large cedar chest across the room. "I didn't want you getting dirt on my sheets."

The prince sank back into the pillows, relief and confusion and exhaustion all pouring through him. He drew a shaky breath, letting the pine-scented air fill his lungs.

"You'll be weak for some time," the old woman continued, resuming her knitting. "Stay in bed today. Rest. Once you have your strength back, you can tell me where you've come from that would have you collapsing on my doorstep."

The prince did not hear this last part. He'd fallen asleep again, the cup still clutched in his hands.

Later, he was not sure how much time had passed while he slept. The prince slipped in and out of consciousness as easily as day slips into night. The old woman was always there when he woke, often with food and water, sometimes just with her knitting. He grew used to falling asleep to the gentle clack of her needles, the very slight rasp of the yarn being pulled through the stitches.

"I found you unconscious in my garden," the old woman told him upon one of his awakenings. "You were face down in my cabbages."

The prince did not remember a garden. He just recalled the endless forest, the feeling of his feet sliding over the ground.

"Your pardon," he said. "I became lost some time ago, and I thought I was alone in the forest. I—I didn't see your house."

"My house is well hidden, and the forest isn't friendly to outsiders. You should count yourself lucky that you managed to stumble into it. But where were you trying to get to?"

"I'm not sure. I've never been there before." He cleared his throat. "I must be going soon, though." His hand crept up unconsciously to the watch that hung again around his throat. He'd retrieved it from the cedar chest as soon as he'd had the strength to stand.

The old woman made a dismissive noise. "You can barely walk to the door."

It was true. Each time he woke, the prince would stand and walk as far as he could. It was not very far at all for the first few days, and though he chafed at the delay, he couldn't fathom beginning his journey again so soon. Besides, what was a few more days lost? Nothing, not where he came from.

Eventually, the prince was well enough to leave the small bedroom, though not to leave the house. He often sat with the old woman in her parlor. It was a cozy room. She would sit in the rocking chair beside her large hearth, a cloak that reminded the prince of the night sky hanging off the back of her seat. He sat across from her, beneath a cuckoo clock that hung above the crackling fire. He often watched that clock as its pendulum swung with each moment, the bird crying out the hour. He never saw the old woman wind it.

"You're going to wear a hole in my floor if you keep that up," the old woman chided one evening, as the prince's leg bounced impatiently, sending a thumping tempo through the room. He flushed and stilled, chagrined.

"Young people," the old woman grumbled. "You always need to be moving. Take it from me—sometimes it's good to sit still for a spell."

A laugh burst from the prince, and the old woman gave him a chiding look. "My apologies," he said. "It's just...it's an ironic thing to hear. I've been stuck in one place for so long, now that I'm free of it, I can't imagine staying still."

"That would account for you collapsing in my garden," the old woman said. She liked to bring that up at every opportunity, as though driving home a lesson.

The prince leaned back in his chair, staring out towards the growing dusk. "How did you come to live here?"

"Hmmm. It's a long story."

"I'd like to hear it."

She sighed. "Perhaps a small part. I had many homes once. Castles by the sea, townhouses in soaring cities. This was always my favorite retreat. It was forever here, waiting for me. So, when I lost most everything I had, I knew that this house would serve me. Take it from me, prince, you should always have a plan for when everything collapses around you."

"You sound like my mother," the prince said with a half-smile.

"She must be a clever woman."

The prince grimaced, glancing away. "A little too clever, I think. In the end."

"Ah." The old woman reached across the space between them and patted his hand. Her fingers were warm against his skin. "I'm sorry for your loss."

He nodded but said nothing.

A few more weeks saw the prince well enough to begin his journey again. On what was to be his last morning in the cottage, he woke to find a new set of clothes laid out for him. His old clothes had been beyond repair, and he thought with some regret of the long green scarf his mother had made for him. His pack, though, was still in good condition, and he pulled it from the trunk and checked to ensure everything was there. He slid his new clothes on, letting the watch rest against his breastbone. Then he went to the window, peering out over the green forest beyond, trying to fix the image in his mind. Fear and no small amount of guilt pressed on his shoulders, and though he'd gone to fix what his mother had broken, the prince now wished he could live in this moment forever. Eventually, though, his duty could be put off no more. He hefted his bag and went out into the parlor where the old woman sat. He took his usual chair and leaned forward intently.

"I have nothing with which to repay you," the prince began. "I spent my last coin some time ago."

"Hmph," the old woman grunted, her needles moving steadily. The knitting had grown long since the prince's arrival in her house. "Well, perhaps you can repay me another way."

"How?"

"I seldom venture into the outside world," the old woman said. "It has been a long time since I have heard any word of it. Tell me a story from your country, wherever that may be."

The prince glanced at the cuckoo clock above the fire, then back to the old woman's nimble hands as the needles clacked together. He took a deep breath.

"Very well," he said. "I think I have just the one.

"Once upon a time, there was a kingdom with a wise king and a clever queen. The two ruled fairly for many years until, one sad day, the king died of a sudden illness. The citizens of the kingdom mourned for months, none more so than the queen who had loved her husband as a flower loves the sun. But the kingdom had to continue, and so the queen bore the burden alone. Yet, as anyone will tell you, cleverness untempered by wisdom can be a dangerous thing.

"The queen, having felt the pain of her husband's death deeply, decreed that when she died, whatever killed her should be outlawed from the kingdom. Her decree was spread to every corner of the land, and then subsequently forgotten, as she ruled for many years more. When she was old, with decades behind her, the queen went to bed one night and did not wake."

The prince ceased speaking for a moment, his eyes fixed on the pine-board floor. The old woman glanced up from her work, examining him.

"Is that the end?"

He smiled. "Almost. For, you see, the queen's decree was heard, and it was obeyed. That which had killed her was exiled from the kingdom."

"Old age."

"No. Time."

The needles—the ticking—stopped. The old woman peered up at the prince, who studied her with keen eyes.

"Time left the kingdom and has not returned for a hundred years. The people of the realm did not at first realize the price they would pay for their queen's folly. But when it became clear that every day would be the same, they started to understand. Eventually, the queen's son decided he would leave and seek out Time for himself."

The old woman's eyes narrowed. She set her knitting down carefully. "How did you manage to leave without falling to dust?"

The prince who was a king took the watch from around his neck and clicked it open, revealing the broken glass and unmoving hands of the clock. Wordlessly, he gave it to her, and she turned it over in her gnarled hands.

"Clever as your mother," she muttered, handing it back. He returned it to its place around his neck. When he'd woken without it on his person, he'd thought he was only seconds from death. After all, he had lived a single day for nearly one hundred years. But as the days passed in the cottage and he did not crumble, he began to realize whose house he'd stumbled upon.

"Why are you here?" the old woman asked. There was no anger in her tone: just curiosity and perhaps a bit of sadness.

"I am here to plead for my people. My mother made a grave mistake."

"She accomplished her goal. No one else shall die as she did."

"But they linger on when many would rather go," the king returned. "There are those who have been ill for one hundred years. Every breath is agony, but without Time to take them, they cannot die. There are children who long to grow up, lovers who long to have children." The king closed his eyes, seeing once again the pain on his subjects' faces. He blinked them open to meet the old woman's unflinching gaze.

"Without you, we are all trapped. I have come here to ask you to return and help me right my mother's wrong. Please. My people suffer for the decision of someone long dead."

The old woman sat in silence for some time, the only sound the crackle of the flames in the hearth. The king knew to wait, because Time could not be rushed.

At length, she spoke again. "What of you?"

"What of me?"

"Would you dishonor your mother's memory by breaking her final law?"

The king was quiet for a moment. It was a question he had asked himself often over the past hundred years, and never more so than when he left the kingdom to undo her decree. His mother had done what she thought best at the time. But times change.

"I have thought of my mother every day for one hundred years," he said at last. "For the first ten I loved her, for the next ninety I loathed her."

"And now?"

The king heaved a sigh. "Now, I believe I understand her. I think that might be better than either."

The old woman nodded, looking at him sorrowfully. "I would help you, if I could. But there is a price."

"Whatever it is, I'll pay it."

"Listen before you agree, boy," she said harshly. "Within your kingdom are thousands of lives, trapped in time for a hundred years. If I were to return now, everyone would crumble. So much time rushing in so quickly would destroy everything." She paused, studying him. "All that unspent time needs a place to go."

The king sucked in a breath. "Ah."

"Indeed."

The cuckoo clock on the wall began ticking again, and the king let his gaze drift up to it. He had expected a price, of course. He just hadn't realized it would be quite so high. But there was no one else to pay it, and he could not return empty-handed.

He turned back to the old woman, who watched him carefully. "I will pay it. I will take their time."

The old woman's eyes softened. "You would give up all your days for them?"

"It is all I have to give. Besides, I've had time enough to mourn a life unlived."

The old woman nodded once more. With a flourish, she bound off the final stitch of her knitting and pulled it straight. It was a scarf, the king realized, black as night and with cables like constellations running its length. She handed it to him, and he wrapped it around his neck. The wool prickled against his skin.

"I will come with you," she said. "We will right this wrong together."

The prince swallowed and nodded. He stood, hefting his pack, but the old woman's hand wrapping around his wrist stilled him. She watched him with her ancient, ageless eyes, and he saw in them all that had been and all that would be and all that might be, one day, though not for him.

"Remember what I told you, boy: sometimes it's good to sit still for a spell. You needn't be so eager to sell your life. We will go together, but not today." She smiled, releasing him and gesturing to his chair.

"Let us have another day, you and I. We have time enough for that."

*See J.C. Pillard's story "The Tick of the Clock"
online at Metaphorosis.
If you liked it, leave a comment. Authors love
that!*

Remember to subscribe to our e-mail updates so you'll know when new stories are posted.

About the story

Like many of my stories, "The Tick of the Clock" started with an image: a young man speaking to an old woman, begging for her help. It was a compelling image, but I wasn't sure what he needed help with, which really put a wrench in my plans to turn it into a story.

The idea stewed in my brain until I rewatched the old Twilight Zone episode "Nothing in the Dark," which personifies the figure of Death as a young man and centers around a conversation between him and an elderly woman. I have always liked the idea of anthropomorphic personifications (thank you, Terry Pratchett), and this idea combined with the image in my head. The old woman was not a woman—she was something wearing the figure of a woman. After some more fiddling, I arrived at who she was. Not death, but that which brings it: Time.

Once I had her character figured out, I turned my attention to the young man and how he finds himself with Time. I love strange, liminal spaces, so began the story with the young man—who, it turns out, is a prince—travelling through an endless forest before arriving at Time's cottage.

It was the prince, of course, who was going to be changed by the story, and who was thus the more challenging of the two to write. Time exists on her own terms—she has nothing to learn in the tale. But the prince does. That was probably the hardest part of the story to write: letting the prince come to terms with the curse on his kingdom, and allowing him to make peace with what he must do to break it.

A question for the author

Q: Why do you write speculative rather than realistic fiction?

A: The honest answer is that the ideas I have for stories are nearly all fantastical in nature. I have tried, on occasion, to write realistic fiction, but a speculative element always manages to appear regardless of my intent. In fact, I joke with my friends that I don't write anything that doesn't have a dragon in it—whether real or metaphorical. I find speculative fiction a more liberating place to explore thoughts and ideas, often because I can make abstract concepts more concrete. Beyond that, I spend enough time living in reality as it is: I'm happy to imagine myself in distant lands populated by the beautiful and strange whenever I can.

About the author

J.C. Pillard's parents read her *The Hobbit* when she was six, and she was hooked on fantasy from that point on. When she's not reading or writing speculative fiction, J.C. spends time knitting and running far too many D&D games. She lives at the foot of the Colorado Rockies with her husband and their sweet dog.

www.jcpillard.com, @JCPillard

Genesis

Lisa Short

Anne awoke to a crawling itch behind her ear. It had been months since her subdural alarm had triggered, long enough that she'd almost forgotten what it felt like. *The boys?* Even as she struggled to unwind herself from the bedcovers, then from William's leg that had somehow gotten tangled up in both of hers, she was conscious of a stab of cold annoyance— *the boys aren't my concern any longer.* Still, the habit of years kept her in motion —she emerged victorious from the bed and staggered over to the console, fumbling for the panel switch.

But the message alert wasn't from the creche. She stared down at the text scrolling silently across the screen, eyes uncharacteristically wide.

"Anne?"

She started—she had almost forgotten that William was there. "I have to go," she said over her shoulder, and strode across the room to the untidy heap of her coveralls on the floor.

"What? Now? Why?" His voice had sharpened.

She spared him a glance as she yanked the coveralls up her legs. "Meteorite." She paused long enough to smile thinly at his quick intake of breath. "A skipodder spotted it coming down. It's pretty far out though, so—"

"Can't someone else go?"

She stared blankly at him. "Why should someone else go?" His eyes narrowed and his mouth compressed. *Oh.* "I'm sorry." She tried to inject some regret into it, but her voice sounded mechanical even to her own ears. Perhaps it was better to just be blunt. "I *want* to go, William." She finished fastening up her coveralls and headed for the door.

"Anne, wait—please." The last syllable made her stumble a little, then drag to a halt—William wasn't a man who usually said *please* to anybody. Her fingers actively tingled with her desire to grab the door latch, but she made herself turn around and face him instead.

He hesitated; his mouth had relaxed a little, but his stare was still sharply trained on her face. "Yes?" she said, as patiently as she could manage, though her jaw had begun to ache from the effort of keeping her teeth ungritted.

"I—" His mouth firmed back into a line and he sat up straighter. "You know—I haven't had my kid yet." Anne blinked at him. Had she known that? William was a good fifteen years her senior, one of the second generation of the ark ship *Genesis*'s colonists—the first generation to be born on the planet—as Anne herself was third generation. She might have just assumed he'd gotten that out of the way before she'd ever taken an interest in his personal life, or she might've just not cared enough to think of it at all. "And—I realized that it was well past time—I knew that already, of course. I just—the Outpost. My responsibilities—" Anne nodded, managing to dredge up a little genuine sympathy at last. *Responsibilities* had been the entire reason she'd borne her own child as soon as she'd been medically cleared to do so after puberty. And speaking of responsibilities—she cast a yearning look at the door, which judging from the sudden rigidity of his posture, William didn't miss. "I'd like to have it with you," he finished in a rush.

Anne realized after a second or two that her mouth was actually hanging open and snapped it shut. There was always a list of names posted at the creche, of men looking to fulfil their own responsibility to produce a child for the Outpost; Anne had borne a second child for one of them, as soon as her first had been weaned. She had imagined her proactivity in doing so would spare her ever being confronted with a scene like this.

But William was undeterred. "I know you've already had two, but you haven't opted for sterilization yet." She started to nod impatiently, then stiffened up herself. "And yes, I *did* look at your medical history—I have the clearance to do it." There was the William she knew, the Outpost Commander at his most autocratic—irritation had steadied his voice and squared his shoulders at last. "I had a good reason. The mother of my child—"

"—is *not* going to be me. Ever. My God, how could you think I'd go through all that again?"

"You had easy pregnancies—"

"Easy!" She stared at him. "I see you did read my medical records," she said after a pause, dryly. "And you're right." She had hated the pregnancies, every second of them, but they weren't the reason she'd been so relieved to be done with the whole business. "But I didn't opt *out* of sterilization. I just hadn't gotten round to it yet." There hadn't seemed any urgency—though obviously she'd been wrong about that. "I'll schedule it as soon as I get back from the salvage site."

Anything else he had to say was cut off by the door slamming shut behind her. Anne broke into a jog down the corridor outside her quarters, rounded the corner, then stopped in her tracks—she had gone the wrong way; the whole debacle with William had set her feet mindlessly down the corridor in the direction of the creche instead of the skipod hangar.

Creche-side, the Outpost was nearly close enough to touch one of the ramshackle rock formations that littered the surface outside. While the planetary weather system was mostly as bland and featureless as its terrain, the occasional dust storm had been destructive enough to make locating the creche in the most protected area of the Outpost the obvious choice. The hangar, filled with skipods requiring unimpeded access to the planetary surface, had needed to be built on the opposite side.

Anne reversed course, but didn't slow her pace; while it seemed unlikely that William would go so far as to suspend her access to the hangar, she hadn't thought he'd try to talk her out of going, either. But the hangar doors opened for her without protest. She squeezed between the rows of waiting skipods, their long cylindrical bodies gleaming black under the high bay lighting. The feel of the exterior hatch rungs in her hands was positively pleasurable—it had been a long time, *too* long—she scrambled easily up her own skipod's curved hull, balancing atop it just long enough to pop the top hatch and slide down into the skipod's interior.

Its cabin was fabricated to match the height of its operator, but was nearly three times as long, a dimly luminescent tube densely packed with control panels, display screens, and sensors. She spent the next twenty minutes running pre-start checks and making sure that her heated compression suit was properly stowed—if the meteorite had churned up the terrain beyond what the skipod's repulsors could handle, she'd have to go outside on foot—then settled herself in the cockpit. The skipod purred to life around her, the vibration almost imperceptible through her cushioned seat. She spun it around neatly and pinged the inner airlock doors, letting the skipod glide toward them on its own stored inertia.

As soon as the inner doors closed behind her, the airlock's lights flickered out, leaving only the display imbedded above the outer doors shining in the claustrophobic darkness. *Pressure 101.3 kPa, Temperature 20.2 °C, Concentration 21% O_2.* The numbers began to drop, slowly at first, then in a whirling blur until they abruptly stilled—*44.7 kPa, -5.1 °C, 6% O_2*—and flickered out, shifting to red letters large enough to fill the display: *PLANETARY ATMOSPHERE.* With a tortured howl audible even through the skipod's muffling walls, the outer airlock doors began to open.

The sky beyond them was nearly unrelieved black, its few small stars twinkling coldly down on the slumped and frozen landscape stretching out to the horizon. Anne barely glanced at it—it never appreciably changed—before folding the cockpit seat away and pulling the exoskeleton up from its floor compartment. She locked her hands and feet into the exo's padded grips, took a deep breath, and broke into a long, loping stride.

The exo's display flared to life, showing her pulse rate and blood oxygen levels along with the power she was feeding the skipod's repulsors. Fully charged, the repulsors were good for eighty hours run time, but it was better to use the exo assist to extend their power reserves. The view from the cockpit swung smoothly northward as another display blinked on, showing the uneven terrain reduced to flat rectangular grids, with a deep orange avatar on the very edge of the screen. The skipod fired its triangulation laser, pulled the meteorite's estimated trajectory from the Outpost's central data core, then threw up its best guess at its distance beneath the meteorite's avatar.

600 km.

The strong, smooth motion of Anne's arms and legs in the exo faltered.

Theoretically, the repulsors could manage a 1,200-kilometer round trip, though she didn't personally know of anyone ever actually testing that theory out—but she'd have to run the exo twelve hours a day at a minimum to make it. At the skipod's top speed, she might be able to reach the meteorite in three days. *Three days, twelve hours a day every day in the exo—* and then the whole trip to do all over again, just to get back to the Outpost.

But *not going* wasn't really an option either, no matter what William might have said. William himself had shown her the real numbers once, back when he'd been courting her. She grinned humorlessly down at the display. Well, he'd been right about the sort of conversation that would pique her interest, hadn't he? Without a significant increase in the influx of new organic material, the next Outpost generation—not four, three, or even two more down the road, but the *next*—might be the last.

Unbidden, an image of her sons rose behind her eyes. She pushed it away impatiently and turned the skipod further north until its nose was in perfect alignment with the tracking display's route markers, then set off.

Anne pushed the skipod all through the night and well into the following day, until *Current Completed Run Distance: 253 km* shone redly down at her from the meteorite's tracking display. She stripped her sweat-soaked coveralls off and chucked them into the skipod's tiny reclaimer unit, then pulled the folded cot out of its side compartment and rolled onto it, eyes already closing.

Anne dreamed of her sons. She tried to fight the dream off, even sleeping—they were alive and well, her waking mind knew; she'd have been informed if they were otherwise. There was no reason for her to dream of them now.

But her waking mind was not in control and the dream gradually swallowed her whole. Memories of that first childbirth, red with agony, followed by the cessation of pain so acute it was nearly ecstasy, morphing into the gray drudgery of the work assigned to nursing mothers, the dull ache in her neck and shoulders that never seemed to subside, and the grinding buzz of her subdural alarm pulling her back to the creche, every hour on the hour—*the baby is awake—the baby is hungry—*

The waking Anne had forgotten most of those details, had deliberately forgotten them; the waking Anne saw no reason to dwell on things that couldn't be helped, that were past and unchangeable. Like the way her sons had screamed after her as she'd left the creche for the very last time, her body oddly weightless as she stepped through its doors, empty of pregnancy, of milk, of children's hands clinging to hers—

The blare of the six-hour alert she'd set on the skipod's panel kicked her into sluggish consciousness. Moving stiffly, she dug a tube of organic concentrate out of the stores and washed it down with some water, then clambered back into the exo.

But by the time the sky had begun to lighten once more through the skipod's viewports, she had to stop again. She untangled herself from the exo and collapsed onto her knees, forcing herself to breathe slowly and deeply. Vomiting directly into the skipod's reclaimer unit was a dicey proposition at best, and a lifetime of conditioning to never waste organic matter of any description did fierce battle with the nausea of dehydrated overexertion. Conditioning won; she finally crawled back onto the cot, pausing only long enough to hook one of the skipod's hydration needles to her bare arm before collapsing into unconsciousness, thankfully dreamless this time.

When she awoke, the pallid sun was sinking below the bottom edge of the skipod's viewports. From her vantage point she could see the tracking display, shining in the gloom of the skipod's interior—*Current Completed Run Distance: 407 km: 125 km to target.* At least the skipod's laser had finally found something to bounce back from, more likely than not her meteorite. Her hands shook as she curled her fingers around the exo's grips; there were deep tremors in her legs, and the muscles in her arms and back screamed as she pushed off once more.

She had set the skipod to retarget the meteorite every fifteen minutes, pinging her subdural implant with each successful attempt. Her eyes mechanically shifted from console to displays to the skipod's viewports, then lingered on the last—the endless, monotonous sweep of lumpy, grayish-brown terrain under the skipod's floodlights was hypnotic.

The skipod jerked—it righted itself immediately, but Anne snapped out of her haze of fatigue and realized, with a surge of panic, that the skipod hadn't pinged her for far too long. She found the skipod's tracking display and stared at it in shock—the meteorite's avatar was *gone*.

Anne wrenched her hands out of the exo's grips and slammed them palms-down on the console, fingers moving so fast across the panels they blurred. *Lost signal*, the skipod insisted, and Anne's stomach lurched. Diagnostics menus flashed past beneath her frantic hands, then she sagged back in the exo's frame, lightheaded with relief. The signal *was* still there—it was just buried in the background noise of the terrain itself, which had somehow increased three orders of magnitude over what it had been at the journey's start.

It was *there*, that was all that truly mattered. She quickly reprogrammed the laser to take a full baseline reading of the terrain. After several minutes, the console beeped and her gaze darted back to the tracking screen. *New baseline established,* it informed her serenely. *New target acquired.*

"What?" Anne muttered, hunching over the console. "I don't want a new target, I want the *old* target—"

Existing target: 51 km. New target: 7 km. The now-familiar, irregularly shaped lump of the meteorite's avatar shimmered into existence on the rescaled display, quickly followed by another, larger shape, strangely symmetrical on two sides and only one grid square away from the skipod. Anne recalibrated the laser for analysis and once more fired a pulse out into the darkness. Minutes later, the display threw up a barrage of text. *New target composition: ALUMINUM. TITANIUM. GRAPHITE. FULLERENE (C60). FULLERENE (C80)*—she stopped reading even as the letters continued to scroll past.

The fates of two of the ark ship *Genesis*'s four original Outpost automated base units were well known. The first one had soft-landed sixty years ago, right where it was now—*home.* The second had come down some forty kilometers southeast of that—*not* softly, and its organic remains had been the main reason their own Outpost had survived as long as it had. But no skipodder had ever found so much as a trace of the other two Outpost base units, and they had never been able to afford the high risk of permanent organic resource loss to the Outpost by going out blindly searching for them. Every time a skipodder failed to return from a salvage run, the Outpost's projected overall population survival trended a little further downward—and the farther out the trip and the less certain the target location, the more likely that was to occur.

Every skipodder had memorized what the analyses results from an Outpost's original, unadulterated hull might look like. Their own Outpost's outer hull no longer read like that, of course; they'd long ago stripped every atom of carbon out of it and fed them into the fabricators. But every skipodder knew what to look for, and that was what was scrolling past Anne's unbelieving eyes now.

Anne ran an integrity check over her heated compression suit and rebreather helmet one last time, then stepped out of the skipod's rear hatch onto the uneven, rocky ground. Fifty meters away was the raised lip of what the skipod thought was the leading edge of a ravine, with the new target buried behind it. She hurried over to it, as fast as she dared without risking a trip and fall that might damage her suit. Easing herself up the lip, she gripped its top edge and hauled herself the last meter or so to its top.

The sheer scale of the wreckage that met her eyes baffled her first attempt to even comprehend it. The uncrushed half of the tortuous metal behemoth embedded in the ravine below her was easily twice the size of the entire Outpost. Stretching out from that strange, sinuous metal body were two arching arms, reaching blindly for the ravine's wall. What might have once been matching arms on its other side were now nothing more than mangled debris littering the ravine floor.

But whatever it was, it wasn't an Outpost, living or dead—she didn't know which she'd hoped for more, but it hardly mattered now. Her nose and eyes stung sharply, her breath hitching hard in her chest—*stop it!* she snarled at herself. *It's still a* partly *organic thing, a* salvageable *thing; more of us can come back, with better tools*—the truth of that calmed her and she began to pick her way down the ravine wall. Whatever it was, it had crashed a long time ago—though obvious traces of the burning rage of its descent remained, the jagged, blackened chasm it had gouged in the planetary surface had long since refrozen into the dead stillness of the rest of the terrain.

Anne lost her footing halfway down the ravine—arms windmilling for balance, she barely managed to skid the rest of the way down on her feet rather than her rear end, and finally staggered to a halt directly under one of the wreck's massive, unbroken arms. The light from her headlamp reflected back a sharp white glare from its metal arch overhead—*what?* She stilled, and the headlamp's beam froze in place on the underside of the arch. She hadn't been imagining it—there *was* something etched into the battered hull, in letters so large she hadn't quite realized what they were at first. Anne craned her neck back as far as it would go in the compression suit.

G…E…N…E…S—

No, she thought stupidly.

She knew, *everyone* knew that the *Genesis* itself had never been intended to land. The Outpost's central data core had always been vague on what exactly had happened to the *Genesis* after the colonists had abandoned it, and it hadn't mattered anyway—the *Genesis* had been too decrepit to take them back home again, and that was all anyone had cared about. She'd said as much to William once, in the early days of their relationship, after overhearing an argument about its possible fates. But William, with his Command access to the restricted parts of the Outpost's central data core, had told her that it had mattered, because the first colonists had originally intended to use it as a *satellite*, a concept he'd then had to explain to her. It would have helped them out a great deal, he'd said, in tracking the precious meteorites that so infrequently struck the planetary surface, in communicating with scavenging skipodders—perhaps in even more ways they'd never had a chance to explore. But the *Genesis* had never responded to any attempts at contact with its automated onboard systems.

It must have crashed soon after the Outpost itself had landed—nobody would have noticed what must have been a visually spectacular descent, or cared even if they had, in those first, difficult years. An almost superstitious awe gripped her as she stared up at it. *This* was the *Genesis*—their progenitor, this dead monstrosity that had carried them all here and then spat them all out onto this sterile hellscape to die—

A flicker of movement on the very edge of her periphery, the faint reflected gleam of light at an angle her headlamp couldn't possibly have reached, alerted her too late. She started to turn around, but before she had time to do more than shift her weight from one foot to the other, something exploded with agonizing force against the back of her helmet and all the lights abruptly went out.

Anne's first conscious awareness was of pain—her head throbbed mercilessly and something had dried to a tacky, pulling unpleasantness on the back of her neck. She automatically reached back, then froze when her fingers encountered not the edge of her rebreather helmet, but her own matted hair.

She pried her eyes open, squinting in anticipation, but the light surrounding her was dim, strangely yellow, filtering down from somewhere far above. She tried to tilt her head back to look, but her stomach revolted at even that tentative movement; she stilled, breathing deeply through her nose, waiting for the nausea to subside.

"You're probably concussed," said a harsh, grating voice. "Sorry about that—but better concussed than et, eh?" Faint aspirating sounds followed that remark—*laughter*? Anne's eyes snapped fully open as she struggled upright. A wild look around revealed weirdly bent walls, stretching upward into the gloom, and scattered pieces of what might once have been machinery—and a man crouched down barely a meter away from her, completely naked, staring intently at her from small black eyes lost in a sea of wrinkles.

Anne fought for analytical detachment in the face of her hindbrain's bewildered terror. He was old, clearly, but more than that, something else was wrong with him, like nothing she'd seen before—the quantity of loose flesh hanging off his face and the one skinny arm he'd raised to point at her were grotesque. She hoped she didn't look as revolted as she felt; if he'd been the one that had hit her over the head, she should probably try to not do anything to make him want to hit her again.

He wheezed laughter again. "Stinks in here, don't it?" Apparently he had noticed her disgust, but hadn't successfully deduced its cause. "I know where you're from, girlie—we've had a few of you wander in here, over the years. Most of who's left is too stupid to ask questions first and et later—I gave up trying to convince 'em after the last one, I don't remember how many years ago it was. But you know, the others was all men—I seen you and I could tell you was a woman, and I—" His voice choked off abruptly. "Maybe they *wouldn't* just et you first, and I—*I didn't want to see it!*" He shrieked the last, then looked around in obvious terror —but the silence that fell around them after the echo of his shout faded remained unbroken, and his bony shoulders relaxed.

Anne hadn't known it was possible to understand every word someone else was saying, yet not have the faintest idea what they were talking about. Something about a *smell,* had been the first thing he'd said —she inhaled cautiously through her nose. It wasn't any worse than the interior of her skipod after a full day's run—but this wasn't a skipod, inhabited for only short bursts of time and unable to support the sort of hourly reclamation cleaning intended to capture and recycle every last molecule of organic waste for recycling. "Why does it smell so, ah..." She trailed off, still wary of offending him. "Is there something wrong with your reclaimers?"

The old man jerked, startling a flinch out of her. "Wha—ha! Reclaimers? This is a *spaceship*, girlie! We wasn't ever supposed to be awake long enough to need *reclaimers*." Suddenly his eyes flooded with tears. "Wasn't ever supposed to be—I been awake aboard for a long time all right, a long time—" His voice caught.

Anne was briefly swamped with unwanted pity, and something else—*not ever supposed to be awake long enough* —"Were you—" It seemed impossible, but the old man stiffened, his eyes nearly vanishing in his wrinkles. "Were you... part of the crew? The *original* crew?"

His face pinched and he drew back from her, though his stare didn't leave her face. "And what if I was?" His voice was like broken glass.

She finally understood the extremity of his appearance, though. He wasn't ill; he was simply *old*. Not old as she had always known it, in the Outpost's earlier generations—the thinner, stringier, but still vigorous activity of early- to mid-sixties, before productivity declined to the point where personal organic consumption was no longer justifiable, and the pressure to voluntarily enter the Outpost's reclaimers began—but *old*. Eighty years old? *Ninety?* She was finding it hard to comprehend him at all as a living, breathing human being—his impossible age, his filth, his hair a wild explosion cascading over his shoulders instead of trimmed short and fed into the reclaimers. Yet there he squatted before her, irrefutable.

But if there weren't any reclaimers on the *Genesis*—and *no reclaimers* probably meant *no fabricators* too—"Didn't you—did you have any supplies at all, when you first landed?"

"Some," he grunted, settling back on his heels. "From when we was *supposed* to be awake on board looking at all the different planets we was *supposed* to fly past, to see which ones was best suited for a colony. All the different planets, ha!"

He spat out the last syllable. "When we all woke up three thousand years too late, out in the emptiness between the stars, no planets, *nothing*—"

Anne knew the story. The old records in the Outpost's central data core indicated that the Genesis's crew hadn't spent much time trying to figure out exactly how or why they had drifted so incredibly far off their planned course—they had been far more interested in *where*, and that answer had been terrible. Somehow the *Genesis*, instead of heading up the Milky Way's Orion-Cygnus spiral toward the galactic center, had cut straight across it and away instead, into the flat black void stretching thousands of light-years between its arms.

But that void hadn't been quite as empty as it had first appeared—a few stars had been there, hidden behind the light-absorbing dust clouds scattered throughout it. One of them, a mere light-year distant, had been a yellow dwarf with a single terrestrial planet, and the *Genesis*'s analyses had confirmed an Earth-standard average density and an atmosphere containing non-negligible amounts of oxygen and water vapor. Only one oddity had stood out—the *Genesis* had failed to find any trace of organic compounds in either its surface or atmosphere.

The old man had hunched in on himself, shivering. The air in whatever disused part of the wreckage he had dragged her to was noticeably chilly; Anne was glad of her heated compression suit. She cast a quick look around for her helmet and spotted it just a meter or so away, an ugly crack running down its crown. It would still be better than nothing, if she could just get back outside the ship—she inched toward it, keeping a wary eye on the old man. "So," she said, hoping to distract him, and because she found she couldn't help herself, "with no reclaimers—after the supplies ran out and what you said before about, ah, being *et*— I guess that's how you've managed to survive this lo—"

It was the wrong thing to say. He suddenly lunged toward her and she scrabbled sideways and back, ending up as close as she could manage to her precious helmet. *"Don't you judge me!"* he screamed, then clapped his hands over his mouth, casting a terrified look around. Anne took advantage of his distraction to fling herself the last half a meter over to the helmet, shoving it quickly behind her back. After several seconds, he relaxed a little, though he was still glaring at her with an enraged expression so exaggerated it was almost comical.

Anne raised her hands placatingly. "I wasn't—I really wasn't," she said rapidly. "If we didn't have the reclaimers and the fabricators, we'd have probably ended up doing the same thing. I mean, we *do* do the same thing, right? Just with a lot more steps in between the dying, and the..." She trailed off, because the old man was staring at her in unmitigated horror.

His lips flapped, but no words emerged at first. "You," he whispered finally. "You...put each other in the fabricators... to make *food*?"

"Well...yeah, that's what they're f—"

"*That's* not *what they're for!*" he screamed. "You were supposed to use them for the *soil*, to enrich the soil with proper *nutrients* so that *Earth plants* could grow here—you were supposed to make this world *green* like Earth, didn't you know that, why didn't you *do* that? Why —" His voice choked off into great whooping sobs that shook his emaciated frame.

Anne tried to shout over his hysteria, why the original colonists hadn't done that—because they couldn't; because those long-ago designers of the Outpost automated base units hadn't envisioned a world with no plate tectonics, no seismic activity, no moons, no asteroid belts, *nothing* to seed its static, frozen silicate surface, to contaminate the sterile purity of its atmosphere.

But he clearly wasn't listening. Broken words and phrases emerged from between the hands he'd buried his face in—*knew an Outpost was there and thriving, those boys looked healthy enough*—with another lurch of nausea she finally realized that she now knew the fate of at least a few of the Outpost's lost skipodders over the decades. *Thought someday they'd ALL come here and save the KIDS, the poor little KIDS!*—she really didn't want to know what that meant, and was just about to risk climbing back up to her feet when his head jerked up and he fixed her with a look of cunning so grotesque that she physically recoiled.

"You know why the others keep me alive, girlie?" His tone was suddenly, weirdly conversational. "Ain't nobody else left who knows how to run the ship's reactor—I was engineer's mate. No fancy education but they took me on 'cause my wife wanted to go too. So I done it, I kept the reactor in good shape even though—even though—" His chin shook as if palsied, then stiffened again. "Because if I *didn't*, I knew the reactor'd blow. I knew the Outpost was close enough for men to reach us—it *could* blow, and then maybe it'd wipe out *all* the life in the Outposts too, the *good* life, the *civilized* life, not just this *HELLHOLE*—" He shrieked the last up, into the shadowy dimness above them that Anne's eyes couldn't quite penetrate. His attention returned, abruptly and fanatically focused on Anne's face. "But now I *know*, girlie. You ain't any different from us at *all*. I should've just let the others put you to work on your BACK bearing the next generation of *DINNER!*"

A shout, a harsh bark of sound, echoed from somewhere outside their cavernous space—the old man's eyes, already wild, lost what little sanity they'd had left. With an agility Anne would never have thought him capable of, he whirled around and fled; Anne scrambled to her own feet, staggering as her numb legs tried to collapse under her, then froze as a long shadow fell across the floor where the old man had been seconds before. Instinctively she flung herself backwards, rapping her already sore head on a panel leaning drunkenly against the wall—she darted behind it, jamming as much of herself as would fit into the narrow space behind it.

Seconds later, someone shuffled into view, shaggy head swinging back and forth on a neck invisible beneath snarled layers of beard. He was as naked as the old man had been—she supposed all the clothing had worn out long ago—but far younger, maybe even younger than Anne herself, though it was impossible to tell for sure under all the hair and filth. *Not* someone she was likely to be able to fight her way free of—Anne hunched in as tightly as she could behind the panel.

After several excruciating minutes, he turned around and ambled back the way he'd come. As soon as he was out of immediate sight, Anne eased out from behind the panel and pressed herself back against the wall—she could still see him, making his way towards what a quick look around seemed to confirm was the only visible exit in this vast space. With a spasm of pure adrenaline terror, she remembered what the old man had said before he'd fled—was it possible he'd gone to destroy the ship's reactor? Who knew how insane he had already been even before he'd happened across her, and how much further he'd cracked now?

In spite of the chill air, she was sweating—her palms were so soaked with it that perspiration squeezed out of her compression gloves and trickled down the rebreather helmet now clutched tight in her hands. She forced herself to breathe slowly and evenly as she crept across the floor towards the doorway that the shambling hulk was just disappearing through. If he happened to look back over his shoulder—if he *saw* her—

But he didn't look back, and she trailed after him, as far behind as she could manage without losing sight of him entirely. The exit led into a narrow corridor choked with debris, blackened wires dangling at odd intervals from its torn plating. It was only irregularly lit, by long, yellowed tubes—she was glad of it; she would be at least a little harder to see, hugging the wall as she was. Then he suddenly vanished from sight—he must have turned a corner that she couldn't see yet.

She dared to step up her pace then. As she drew nearer to where he'd turned, she started to hear something, sounds—faint and muffled, but getting louder—*voices*? Anne had the uneasy, crawling certainty that she was heading the wrong way, deeper into the bowels of the *Genesis*, but she didn't know what else to do. If she backtracked to the room she'd awakened in and failed to find another exit, and ran into yet another wandering resident—

She finally reached the bend in the corridor. A lightning-quick peek around the corner confirmed that the corridor beyond it sloped in both directions. The muffled voices were coming from the downward slope; Anne leaned back against the very edge of the turn and angled her head as far back as she could to see the upslope. She couldn't make out more than a few meters of it; it might be nothing more than a dead end.

There was no reason to look the other direction, though—she could hardly go that way anyway, towards the voices and almost certainly where the shambling hulk had gone. *You don't have to look—* she found herself peering around the edge into the corridor's downslope. It opened up abruptly, just beyond the turn, into a room with an oddly familiar layout—*medical bay*? Just like the one in the Outpost—a hot wave of stench struck her in the face and she gagged soundlessly. *You don't have to look!* But she couldn't stop herself from leaning out just a little more, a little farther—*people!* Seven, eight, maybe more—it was hard to see in the gloom—were crouched in various corners or sprawled out on rotted piles of material.

Then a flicker of movement caught her eye. One of them was struggling to his—*her* feet, Anne realized sickly as she turned towards Anne's hidden vantage point, her belly a hard, rolling mound under tiny, flaplike breasts. She couldn't have been more than twelve or thirteen, at most—but Anne had known, of course, as soon as she'd seen how young the second man had been, that the *Genesis* had a breeding population. Or she should have known—

Put you to work on your BACK bearing the next generation of DINNER!

...just like you've done for the Outpost already?

Anne recoiled from that jeering mental voice, almost relieved when an abrupt, metallic rattle drew her attention back to the girl. Anne's gaze followed the sound down to a heavy metal chain wound around the girl's ankle. The other end of the chain was fastened to what appeared to be a...surgical table? Just like the ones in the Outpost, right down to the integrated blood supply unit flashing busily away at its head...so the *Genesis* did have fabricators after all, of a sort. Though the blood supply units were highly specialized fabricators, only able to force living blood cells into temporary, rapid replication, and they were just as restricted as any fabricator in their inability to produce an organic substance without an organic raw material—and more restricted than most, as the only organic source they were able to utilize was a living patient's own tissue. But the lower half of the table appeared to be empty—as her eyes adjusted to the noisome, flickering dimness, she was finally able to make out what it was that was strapped down at the table's head, nearly lost beneath countless quivering coils of intravenous tubing. Something far too small for its fragile, sticklike legs to reach even halfway down the table's length—

Anne bolted for the upsloping corridor, not even trying to muffle the impact of her suit's heavy boots on the floor plating. Deafened by the pounding, roaring thunder of her own pulse in her ears, she didn't know if anyone was coming after her—they had to have heard her by now—but all she could do was flee, blinded by the unstoppable tears that scorched her eyes like acid. The corridor steepened sharply, turning into the stuff of nightmares, each bounding leap wrenched back by gravity, as if she were running through a thick, invisible sludge.

She rounded the next turn at top speed and nearly slammed into a hard, unforgiving but unbelievably familiar sight —an inner airlock door, so like any of the dozens in the Outpost that for a long, crazy second she wondered if she was hallucinating it. But no, of course it looked the same—it *was* the same—the *Genesis* and the Outpost had been designed and built together. Skidding to a halt, she jammed the rebreather helmet down on her head, then clawed the airlock's manual override panel open.

There was a gap, a sizeable one, between the edge of the outer airlock door and the lip of the ravine. She backed up a few steps, then ran and blindly jumped and somehow found herself on her hands and knees on the other side. Her ankle throbbed brutally—she must have twisted it without realizing it, but she staggered back up onto her feet anyway and hopped-ran to the skipod, still sitting fifty meters away from the ravine's edge, serene and unmolested.

Her hands shook so badly that she couldn't get the rear hatch open—her back crawled, jittering, but she didn't dare pause working on the hatch to look behind her. Finally, the hatch hissed open and she flung herself inside. As it closed behind her, she wrenched off her helmet and compression gloves and scuttled across the interior on her knees to the front console. She slumped down into the cockpit's cushioned seat as the onboard systems swung the skipod back in precisely the same direction they'd come from. *Back, back, go, RUN*—the repulsors hummed and the skipod shot forward, away from the *Genesis*.

A bare moment later, a tremor rocked the skipod. Anne stiffened in her seat, gaze darting to the skipod's rear camera display. A flicker of movement against the sky above the ravine—she rubbed her eyes hard. She might have imagined it—it was colorless, faint, more like a puff of vapor than anything else. *A puff of vapor—* the first faint exhalation of a reactor core with all its safety systems stealthily taken offline...?

You ain't any different from us at all.

"We are different," she whispered, into the skipod's warm, dim silence. "We *are* —"

Her own voice, answering: *I mean, we* do *do the same thing, right? Just with a lot more steps in between—put you to work on your BACK bearing the next generation of DINNER!*

Duty, ever since she could remember— the duty to survive and reproduce, *just enough* so that there would be someone left for Earth to find and save someday, as everyone knew they would because they *had* to, because otherwise their entire existence was nothing but a slow and pointless death. And if not in time to save *them,* their *children* or their *children*'s children or—

She had never wanted to bear those children. She had fought a grim, years-long battle to care as little for them as possible. She had known other people felt differently about their own duty, their *own* children, and many of them had disliked her for it. And William in particular had misunderstood her entirely. Though she supposed she couldn't blame him—she hadn't understood herself, not really. Not until now.

Anne switched off the rear camera display and huddled in the cockpit seat. She couldn't just stay there, though; the skipod couldn't make it back to the Outpost without the exo assist. It was going to be a close-run thing even with it. Though maybe it didn't matter anyway. That puff of vapor—*and then they'd ALL come here and save the KIDS, the poor little KIDS!*

Anne forced herself to her feet, broke down the cockpit seat, and raised the exoskeleton in its place with hands that felt like they belonged to someone else. She had to at least try to get back to the Outpost. William would want to *save the kids*, and salvage the remains of the *Genesis*, too. With all that new organic influx, those ugly numbers, the Outpost's organic supply versus consumption curve, would level out once more...almost. For a while.

The tremor that shook the skipod that time was impossible to ignore. Anne closed her eyes, locked her hands and feet in the exo's implacable grasp, and pushed forward blindly into the night.

See Lisa Short's story "Genesis" online at Metaphorosis.
If you liked it, leave a comment. Authors love that!
Remember to subscribe to our e-mail updates so you'll know when new stories are posted.

About the story

The crosstrainer (as opposed to the stationary bike or treadmill) has always been my cardio gym equipment of choice, and one day, as I was on it, I was thinking about cross-country skiing (which the crosstrainer somewhat mimics)—for whatever reason, I started imagining a woman, inside a vehicle that operated similarly to that, alone and traversing an icy plain at night. On an alien world? Definitely an alien world! But why? Because, I thought, there might be limits on the amount of charge such a vehicle could store, and it would need the operator to put in some effort because of that... if one had to travel long distances... but why the need to travel long distances? And why limitations on the fuel? Our current vehicles are primarily fueled by hydrocarbons...ah ha, I thought. No fossil fuels. A world that had never evolved life wouldn't have fossil fuels in the first place.

No hydrocarbons... wait—what if there wasn't any carbon at all?

While I'm no kind of geologist, I do know that the primary sources of carbon on the Earth's surface are either from outside Earth (via asteroids, meteors, etc.) or from within the Earth (from seismic shifts, volcanic eruptions, etc.). What if you had a planet with no seismic activity, one essentially alone in the depths of space—no asteroid belts in its system, as far from a galactic arm or the galactic center as you can realistically get, with no carbon dioxide in its atmosphere either? You'd have a world with no carbon, and therefore no ability at all to be life-bearing, neither of its own accord nor even artificially induced by humanity, not sustainably. How would a community of people survive under those conditions? Well, they would still have access to one reproductive source of carbon... still unsustainably over the long term, of course. But they could survive. For a while. With extreme changes in their social structuring to accommodate an existence built entirely around cannibalism...

A question for the author

Q: What work of art has been the most inspiring for you?

A: No one particular work of art, but when I was eight years old, my mother and I moved in with the man who would become my stepfather a year or so later. His closets were a treasure trove of comic books and speculative fiction paperbacks (which was definitely a huge influence on me as a writer!) but the thing that first caught my eye about his house were the posters he had taped up all over the walls. Prints by Frazetta, Vallejo, and more were plastered over every square inch, depicting mighty warriors, monstrous beasts, spaceships with guns blazing... I was enchanted, and whenever I had trouble falling asleep right away at night, I would think of one of those prints and a story about it. Who were they? What were they fighting for? What alien or fantasy world had they sprung from? Many of the stories I still write today took their earliest inspiration from some of those prints.

About the author

Lisa Short is a Texas-born, Kansas-bred writer of fantasy, science fiction and horror. She has an honorable discharge from the United States Army, a degree in chemical engineering and twenty years' experience as a professional engineer. Lisa currently lives in Maryland with her husband, two youngest children, father-in-law, and cats. She is a member of the Horror Writers Association and a Futurescapes 2021 alumnus.

www.lisashortauthor.com, @Lisa_K_Short

Tell the Crows I'm Home

Laurel Beckley

There is a place where the lost go to be found.

It is a small farm tucked into a bend in Highway 38, between Scottsburg and Elkton—two towns barely on a map, and even less so after the earthquake shattered much of the West Coast. Once, this road was a bustling thoroughfare from the interior of the state to the coastal towns of Reedsport and Winchester Bay. Now it sits empty, giving more and more of itself to the hungry river it parallels.

The farm is nestled in a broad gap between the road and the river, hidden by swathes of shallow-rooted white oak, whose thick strands of sea-foam lichen and brown moss create their own ecosystems, creating space for the ferns and the birds and the insects, although there are fewer of all of those, now.

Nicole tends this farm, same as she has for the past forty years. She inherited it through a twist of fate and negligence after her parents passed, and then kept it with the stubbornness of a disowned queer child still tending old hurts. She replaced the hard memories with new ones, slowly rehabilitating the structures of her home and her soul.

The first few years were hard: relearning the lost skills of childhood, accepting the weird things found in her pockets and glove box and shoes, navigating the conservative mindsets of her neighbors—who knew the reasons for her leaving and still disagreed with her lifestyle upon her return. Life got a little easier as muscle memory took over and the collective current turned grudgingly towards acceptance.

What never changed was being viewed as an outsider. Ten years away transformed her into a stranger, despite being practically immortalized for a high school track record that remains unbroken nearly fifty years later.

The gym with her record etched onto the walls flooded in the quake of '22, erasing history but not memory. The football field and high school have been reclaimed since the flood, but the town dwindles with each passing year.

Those old enough to remember Nicole's parents have died off or moved on to nursing homes in Roseburg or Cottage Grove or Eugene. Most of Nicole's former classmates left when the nearest hills were stripped in the first gasping resuscitation of the after, when everyone scrambled to take what they could while they could, before the fires devoured everything or another quake hit or the Yellowstone caldera finally blew or another recession or, or, or. The reasoning was endless and short-sighted. Consideration of replanting and maintenance vanished, along with the northern spotted owls and the wineries and the frogs and the Roosevelt elk.

Nicole stayed, even as the years passed and friendships eroded and the pile of lost things grew. She stayed, though each winter the river takes a swallow of asphalt, another gulp of concrete and mud sluicing off the hillside into the brown water below, until the highway is barely passable by car, no matter what season. There are no funds to repair infrastructure, much less to fix a road leading only to graves and ruin.

It has been ten years since the last clear-cut, and life is slowly returning to the hills north of Highway 38, beyond Nicole's farm. Spindly Douglas fir compete with red-bark madrone and scrub. Hidden trilliums emerge in the spring-time deep in the groves of mixed forest old-growth, and sometimes she finds shooting stars in the middle of July. Their vibrant purple headdresses and black-tipped noses give her small bursts of joy, tiny pockets reminding her that while the air pollution is high and the temperature scorching, life continues. Life will continue, even after the end, because nothing truly ends. And that is a small comfort.

Despite her isolation—with the road conditions and few connections to the rest of the world, the five miles into town is a day-long excursion, never mind the hurdles she must jump to arrange transportation to the nearest grocery store in faraway Sutherlin—Nicole is not lonely. Nor alone.

Finders are never alone.

This is what she tells herself.

This is what she has told herself for so long she believes it.

There is a routine to the seasons, and to the things she finds, and she's fallen into the rhythm of her life without quite realizing the rut she's dug.

Each October, a new band of Canadian geese arrive dazed and confused and diverted, and depart happily fat in April. April is also kitten and cat season, when mamas have babies and humans abandon the fanged teenaged terrors they had assumed were cuddly fluffballs. Dog season is year-around; runaways fleeing the terrors of a thunderstorm or wanderers ditched by their masters, for whatever reasons people leave their furred family members.

Nicole finds them all, save for the crows, who do not appear to be bound to the rules of the farm, and come and go as they please. Like Nicole, a crow is never lost.

She used to have quite a few human visitors, back when the world was only half broken. And a variety. More than one flying craft has made an emergency landing in the narrow, flat field that used to provide hay but now lies untouched. After the sixth time a lost pilot insisted they were in a different region of the county, Nicole learned to keep a map handy in her tractor or a back pocket, just in case. Summer was for lost kayakers and inner tubers, back when folks floated for fun. They'd put in around the high school to catch the rapids and came ashore on the lower pasture's pebbled beach convinced they'd arrived at Umpqua Myrtle State Park.

Her wife, rest her soul, stumbled upon the farm by chance after taking a wrong turn in 2006 while searching for a bed and breakfast in Scottsburg. It was raining, and late winter, and the banks of the river were rising. Nicole invited this stranger inside, and Christine never left until the day she took her last breath, two years before the quake.

Even now, a traveler might get caught out late at night, far from where they are meant to be, and see Nicole's porch light through the trees—a trick of the eye or the vegetation, as her house is guarded by a stand of fir and oak and hedges. She always keeps the guest bedroom ready, and has grown to read the signs of a new arrival's approach. She knows, with bone-deep intuition, if the visitor will go, or if they might linger a while.

Some visitors, like Christine, stay longer than a night. Some find what they are looking for, but most don't. Eventually, they depart, and never return.

Nicole stays, and she waits for her next visitor, even as the years stretch on and on, and the ache of loneliness morphs into something else. She knows there is a world out there, but she has convinced herself the larger world is not her purpose. She stays so she may find the lost and missing, like a lighthouse along a dark stretch of shore, a stationary point for the lost to be found, to reorient themselves and move on, in whatever way moving on means. Christine used to tease her about being a witch, but that's not accurate. Lighthouses are not magic, and neither is she. They just are. Nicole is a finder and crow-friend and sometime farmer and old woman in the woods, and that is enough.

This is what she tells herself.

It is early fall in Douglas County. The first snap has hit, a wet cold that seeps through clothes and penetrates deep. Nicole's root cellar and pantry are well stocked for the winter, although her arthritis has turned screwing lids into an ordeal, and her hip aches when she sits or stands or sleeps or moves.

This morning she found a set of car keys from a Mercury Cougar in her left house-slipper, and there's a white-tailed deer in the barn, sleeping between two milking goats. It raises its weary head when she arrives, blinking in exhaustion and covered in soot and ash. The nearest fire is fifty miles away, and its smoke has traveled to the valley, layering everything with a hazy smog that brings brilliant sunsets and displaced wildlife.

Nicole admires the deer's antlers as she feeds her small flock. First the cats, because they demand to be first in everything. Then the crows, who really should be first but who understand the cats in ways no other animal should. Then the goats, who eat and are milked, as much as it pains Nicole's hands—a part of her wishes another runaway teen would arrive, not because she wants to put in the emotional energy of caring for a sullen and scared and bewildered child, but because she wouldn't mind someone else doing the milking or morning feeding —and lastly the dogs and whoever else has wandered in during the night and refuses to feed themselves.

She is about to head into the house when a crow swoops, wings brushing her cheek as it lands on her shoulder, clawed feet digging through her jacket. It nuzzles her gray hair and chirps the word for *stranger*.

With a sigh, Nicole trudges out to the front, rubbing the side of her hip, pushing aside a feeling of trepidation. The crow remains on its perch, although its fellows have gathered on the eaves to watch the newcomer.

A car is parked outside the house, which means someone has fixed the roads. The car's engine ticks in the cold, steam rises from the hood. A person huddles against the passenger door, arms wrapped about their stomach, tucking their tan jacket to their body. Their pale face is drawn and tense, as if they are preparing themself for a task. Their brown hair is cropped short, highlighting round cheekbones and thick eyebrows. Their head jerks, eyes widening as Nicole emerges from behind the house.

"Aunt Nicole?"

Nicole's chest tightens. She does not know this person. She's taken in a lot of strays, and only the human children refer to her as *aunt*—the easiest term to explain if anyone questions her foundlings. But none of the children ever return when they finally leave. No one returns. That's the rule, unspoken and unwanted, but there all the same.

The person shoves off the car, shuffling toward her. Their bare hands are still tucked into their armpits. They are in their early twenties, maybe, or they might be forty-five, or thirteen with a stolen car. Nicole is bad at determining ages. At this point, everyone seems impossibly young.

"Um, you don't know me," they say. Nicole's left eyebrow crooks, and their shoulders hunch, as if they are trying to make themself small, either to be non-threatening or to diminish themself before her. "But my mom talked about you. A lot. Jessica? Jessica, uh, her maiden name was Canby?"

Nicole waits. She doesn't remember a Jessica Canby, but she has known a lot of Jessicas. Most of her strays don't have last names, or they give false ones, and often, she recommends they tell her their destination dream, and that becomes their last name. She has known quite a few Austins and Portlands and Harvards.

The person fidgets. "She um, she said a lot of things about you, and I think she was here when she was a teenager? She'd run away from home and you, uh, you gave her a place to stay. I think it was in 2010 or something? I don't expect you to remember—it was a really long time ago." There had been two Jessicas in 2010: Cornell and Seattle. "Anyway, I um, I'm Aubrey, Jessica's daughter. My pronouns are she or they."

Nicole nods, smiles despite her uneasiness. Most times she knows what her visitors will need. A place to sleep, a hug, a cup of coffee to keep going, a map, a spare tire, a band-aid, a locked door, even a quiet morning alone on the porch, listening to the crows and robins talk to each other in the garden. Some just need to be seen and heard. But for the first time in a long while, Nicole doesn't know what this lost person needs, and it scares her. Still. The child is lost, and Nicole knows her purpose. "Come inside, Aubrey. Let's warm you up."

Aubrey fiddles with a peeling strip of paint on the kitchen table, not meeting Nicole's gaze. Aubrey seems fascinated by the table—one of Christine's first furniture renovations, where she transformed the source of so many of Nicole's shitty memories into pure pride—and her finger moves down the red stripe, then the orange, tapping each color of the rainbow. The table was painted before the intersectional flag, and lacks the now-ubiquitous brown, black, white, blue, and pink triangles.

"I'm not lost, you know." *Tap, tap, tap.* "That's what Mom said? That you find the lost."

Nicole's hands tighten around her mug of tea. "Did she, now." The crow, who's followed her inside and hopped from her shoulder to a perch on the sink's edge, clacks its beak. "How is your mom?"

Aubrey winces, and Nicole bows her head. Well.

"I'm sorry," Nicole says. The words are inadequate. They are always inadequate. Most times she finds the right words, but this time the well inside her chest grows, choking off platitudes, and she stays silent.

"She passed away in April. Cancer. It was—it was quick." Aubrey still doesn't meet her eyes. One fingernail continues to worry the red strip, the paint separating further from the laminate. "I tried to keep going. College, chin up, all that shit." Aubrey looks up, gaze fierce. "I'm *fine*."

Nicole nods. Aubrey is very clearly not fine, but Nicole doesn't think she needs comfort.

"She said you were her only family."

"Many do, I imagine. Where did she end up?"

"Pittsburgh." Aubrey breaks a chip away, and bites her lip as the scrap flutters to the ground. "She wanted me to find you. Tell you she, um, she appreciated it."

"That's a long journey." Pittsburgh is a lifetime from here. Dark shadows line Aubrey's bloodshot brown eyes, and she reeks of greasy fast food and unwashed flesh and hard journey. Nicole's instincts tell her to get this child into a bath and then bed, but there is something off. No one has ever traveled here *intentionally*. Not even neighbors, back when she had those. "Did you get lost along the way?"

Aubrey's chin jerks up. Her lip curls. "No. I knew exactly where to go. I always do."

Nicole exhales, long and slow. "I see."

She does not see. She's accepted her place for so long that she's stopped questioning. Reopening that part of her mind is hard, as it involves grappling with concepts and ideas and implications she has buried for decades. She knows her purpose, has accepted her strange gift, and that is enough. She stands up. "You must be exhausted. Let's get you a bath and a nap. We can talk later."

Aubrey sleeps for two days, and when she awakes, she's like the river—pushing beyond her boundaries, slowly carving new places and insights, whittling away at Nicole's reserve and resolve, always hungry for more and more and more. Seemingly determined to shove her history into the past, she follows Nicole, learns how to run the farm, how to prepare for a wet winter or a drought, how to gather the last of the berries and the vegetables. She refuses to talk about returning to college or next steps, but seems content to stay.

She roots through the house, relentless, curious. Over the years, lost items have found their way into Nicole's home: inanimate objects she doesn't recall bringing back but which somehow squirrel into drawers or a back closet or her root cellar, and are then dumped into the guest bedroom and spare closets. Aubrey seeks it all, fascinated by everything from spare change to baby clothes to shipping manifests to credit cards to half-filled day planners to stuffed animals to thirty-day return receipts to cell phones, but it is the stuffed and mounted six-point buck's head that really catches her attention. Nicole has to explain how it showed up on the hood of her car in 2003—or was it 2004? Time is strange—and the explanation drifts into the whole debacle of her attempt to find the trophy's owner.

Aubrey brings order to the clutter, the bits and pieces that were once content to stay crammed into overflowing piles but now seemed to scream for attention, for organization. She even finds the plastic tub filled with old coins, invaluable gemstones, and an ancient dented goblet. "Is this what I think it is?" Aubrey asks, tilting it back and forth, staring at the etchings from an ancient language.

"Most likely," Nicole replies, and Aubrey replaces the goblet into the bin reverently, returns the tub back to its place. She seems to understand that some things are best hidden from prying eyes. Nicole likes that.

But Aubrey's incessant desire to seek grates, and Nicole's unease grows as Aubrey comes to life over the winter, blossoming as the world dies down and the rain-bearing clouds leech color, turning the countryside brown and grey and damp. Having organized the house and the barn and the toolshed—even cleaned out Nicole's rusting solar-converted car—Aubrey crosses the abandoned highway, moves through the woods with the enthusiasm of an explorer, and returns with truffles and mushrooms and late-season elderberries.

Then Aubrey begins venturing into town, navigating her car over impossible gaps and washouts, returning with pizza and canned peaches and secondhand stories of community as December sprawls into January.

"Come with me tonight." Aubrey's breath wisps before her, twining through her hair and cold-chapped cheeks. She has taken over milking duties and many of the more physical chores, completing them before vanishing on her next adventure. She's explored the remnants of Scottsburg, and is now fascinated by the folksy vibes of the townsfolk of Elkton. The apparent ease with which Aubrey moves through the world is irksome and brings up feelings of inadequacy and loss, and yet each time she leaves, Nicole worries. Despite her mixed feelings, Nicole...enjoys this strange person. She likes the company.

"Come where?" Nicole asks, although she already has an idea. She finishes feeding the goats, and massages her stiff hands. Aubrey's back is toward her. Hunched over as the girl is and dressed in Christine's jacket, Nicole can pretend—for a moment—that she is talking to her wife. Then the moment is gone and she is in a barn with a young twenty-something, instead.

"There's a basketball game at the high school." Aubrey turns. Her nose is pink from the January cold, and her cheeks are two round red apples. "It should be fun. You haven't left the farm since I got here. It'll be good to get out."

"I haven't left because you get everything we need." And the thought of leaving scares her. She hasn't stepped foot off the farm or seen a human face that is not Aubrey's since July, and Aubrey's relentless pursuits underscore Nicole's commitment to not leaving her home, solidifying and entrenching her position and reluctance and sense of place. Nicole has told herself the same things for forty years, and will not fathom a paradigm shift, even as the fear of *something* ending burrows deep into her core. She doesn't want to know why Aubrey's presence bothers her so much, because looking means digging deep enough into herself, uprooting her stories and unearthing the passivity of her existence. What will her roots look like? She doesn't want to know.

And yet.

The fact no one from town has come to check on her gnaws on that small place she keeps buried. She's an old woman who's had a strange youngster come along. It should send up red flags among the townsfolk, but then, Nicole is known both for being reclusive and for her mysterious, extended family. Aubrey's words sink in, though. "A basketball game?"

"Yeah. The girls are playing some team from Oakland? They're undefeated. It should be fun?" When she's nervous, Aubrey's up-talk returns, twisting her sentences into uncertainty.

Nicole has no desire to see the people of Elkton or anyone else. "It'll be dark when we return." It's a paltry excuse, and they both know it. Still. She has no idea how Aubrey navigates the roads. Last month she crept to the end of the driveway, and discovered the large washout was still there. It was impossible to drive around, much less over.

Aubrey smiles. "Already covered. Andrea Gardner says we can stay with her."

Andrea Gardner is the granddaughter of Molly Springs, who spat on Nicole in sixth grade and then outed her their senior year. When Nicole returned, Molly welcomed her back into the community, all smiles and acceptance and bygones being bygones and no apologies ever given or faults acknowledged. Nicole did not attend Molly's funeral, claiming the roads were washed out, but really, she has not forgiven her bully. This offer is uncomfortable, but perhaps there is change between generations. And if she bends on this request, perhaps Aubrey will find what she has been seeking.

Nicole tilts her head, and Aubrey's face lights with joy.

Trepidation builds as the day draws on. Nicole tries to push down the feeling this is the last time she'll feed her goats or walk this path or pet a crow or find a wheat penny, that this is the end of something. The emotion she's been suppressing all fall and winter, tamping down alongside all her other fears, bubbles over, churning acid up into her throat. She wants to hold on to everything all at once, and the pain in her chest builds until there is a bowling ball on her sternum, slowly crushing her. It doesn't help that everything she finds is trash—a mummified, half-eaten Snickers bar in her left shoe, someone's Walmart receipt for oranges bought in 2004 crumpled under her hairbrush, a used condom. She gingerly places everything into the trash and spends the rest of the day locked in her bedroom, staring out the window at the crows huddled on the fencepost.

But Aubrey steers her into the car an hour before the game, and glares until Nicole buckles herself in with shaking hands. As her house slips away behind the oaks and the ferns, the fear she'll be unable to return increases. Aubrey taps her on the arm, and points ahead as they bump and jolt down the driveway. The crows are gathered along the branches of the trees, watching them turn onto the pothole-filled highway, wings flapping in farewell.

Nicole closes her eyes as they near the washout, unable to comprehend the how or why or what of Aubrey crossing an impassable gap in the road. She leans forward, pressing her fists against her closed eyes. Purple stars dance against the thin flesh of her eyelids, little shooting stars shouting in fear instead of joy. Each breath is a rasping sob, a half-groaned *I can't*. This cannot be her end. Not now. She is not lost—she is *never* lost—and her home is *for* the lost and those who are found can never return. What if she *can't* go home? She's not lost. She's not *lost*. She's *not*—

"Aunt Nicole, are you—" The car stops. "I'll turn around."

Nicole stays hunched over, trying to breathe through the fear and the pain, until she feels the switch from asphalt to dirt. She holds her breath, peeping between her fingers until she sees her farm, her house, her fields, and all that is familiar yet again. Aubrey taps the brake as the house comes into view, and Nicole launches for the door release. The seatbelt pulls at her midsection, refusing to free her, until Aubrey presses the button and Nicole shoots out of the car, gasping, free, and home.

She presses her hands to her chest, breathing in the familiar air. The crows squawk overhead, wings rustling, and Nicole stumbles forward to lean against an oak. The brown moss squishes and crinkles under her hand, the opposing sensations grounding her. She is *not* lost.

The driver side door opens and closes, and Aubrey edges forward. "I'm sorry."

"Don't be." Nicole can't face her. Can't let her see the fear that's been brewing since September. Fears long dormant, fears she's pushed aside, that have risen and flourished. "It's not your fault."

It *is* her fault. Endings always have beginnings, and this is the beginning of an end.

Nicole is so comfortable here, in her home, where she knows everything and everyone, where she maintains the memories and keeps the lost, and she does not want to leave. She does not want to see people who don't need her or understand her or who keep her at a distance. She does not want to take the chance of leaving, because she might never return. She cannot squash the fear of being replaced by someone who can bridge the gaps she cannot.

Footsteps crunch behind her, and Aubrey's hand presses against her back, tentative and comforting. "You know, when I was little, I never understood how people could get lost. I kept running into people who couldn't find their way, or their keys or their purpose or whatever, and it was so weird. I always, always knew exactly where I was and where to go."

Nicole stays silent, unsure what Aubrey is saying. Unsure how this relates to anything. How this is supposed to soothe her fears.

Aubrey continues, "I didn't know what being lost meant. Then Mom died. I knew exactly where to go, except for the first time there were two paths instead of one. I tried the first and it didn't work because it was the path I'd been going on, and it wasn't mine anymore." She takes a deep breath, releases it. "So I took the second path and came here. And I met you."

Nicole laughs. "And you think I'm lost?" The thought is absurd. The lost come to her to be found. She knows where she is. She always has. She has told this story often enough that she believes it.

"I think there are different ways of being lost." Aubrey's toe scrapes a circle in the dirt. "And, maybe, different kinds of being found?" Another scrape. "I know you're nervous and you've kept yourself isolated here for so long, but I thought—"

"You thought a basketball game would help?" Nicole turns, faces Aubrey. This kid can't be serious.

Aubrey twists her hands together. "No, the basketball game was an excuse. I found your name on the gym wall. For athletic records?"

"The quake flood destroyed everything."

Aubrey crosses her arms over her chest, hugs herself. "Well, turns out there was this sophomore who went digging through the old internet archives. She found the records and convinced the principal to put them back up. And she saw your record and how long it's stood, and she's thinking about trying to beat it." Her eyes dart to the right. "She's a junior now, and going to play in the game tonight, and I thought it might be interesting for her to meet you. Put a face to ancient history."

"Before she erases it."

Aubrey rolls her eyes. "Before she beats a fifty-year-old record! That's huge—for both of you."

Nicole steps back, towards the trees. The fear is back, although now it's competing with irritation and another worry. First the world ended, but everything was fine because Nicole found lost things and made a place for them, or gave them the space to find themselves and move forward. Now Aubrey is here to replace her, and this new child is going to remove her from history completely, never mind that she is erased already. She is a myth, a rumor, the old woman who lives with the strays on an abandoned stretch of highway. She finds the lost and has become lost in return.

Nicole finally sees the trench she has dug for herself. Years upon years of self-soothing stories, of unthinking rhythm and routine, of refusing to look outward, have built a fortress of isolation wrapped in false purpose and a fear of her fiercely protected comfort vanishing in a return to past prejudices. But she also sees that the walls are not so high she could climb out, if she had help.

"Please?" Aubrey asks.

Nicole stares at the branches, at the crows. She rocks side to side, hyper-focused on the black wings, the clacking beaks. They are not agitated, as she had thought. They are reminding her that all things end, and the ending makes space for beginnings. They are telling her there are finders, and there are seekers. There is alone and there is loneliness. There is family and there is community. There is fear and there is courage. There is the past and this is the present. They are saying *happy hunting* instead of *goodbye forever.*

This is a new beginning. A new story she can tell herself, over and over, until she believes it. This time, she will have help in the telling.

Nicole takes a deep breath and gets back into the car.

See Laurel Beckley's story "Tell the Crows I'm Home" online at Metaphorosis.
If you liked it, leave a comment. Authors love that!

Remember to subscribe to our e-mail updates so you'll know when new stories are posted.

About the story

I wrote the first draft of "Tell the Crows I'm Home" in March 2021, when the waves of hopelessness were crashing into me. I'm a bit of a latecomer to all things, so the loneliness of the pandemic was only finally hitting—I had left a stressful, toxic workplace to take some time to write before we moved (again), and was in between projects and packing and in transition. Throughout this shifting, I just felt lost, and I wanted to go home, and home, to me, is Elkton, Oregon, a place I have not lived since I was thirteen. For the first time in a very long time, I sat down at my computer and started writing a mood piece to capture how I felt. I had no plan, I just wrote what I knew and tried to tie my melancholy to a place.

I had somewhat intended the story to be about a payphone that people picked up to listen to the ghosts of their loved ones after a disaster, but it morphed into something else. Nicole emerged from the space between the river and the highway, inspired by Amal El-Mohtar's "Pockets", the myth of the old woman in the woods, and the stories we tell ourselves to cope with loneliness. What I ended up with is (fingers crossed) an intrinsically queer story of acceptance and the breath-catching fear of change and new things, and, above all, hope.

The story takes place in the mid-2030s, in a dystopian world rocked by climate change and the aftermath of The Big One (that Oregon boogeyman that is coming...some day). I have a feeling a lot of people who know me will think this is autobiographical, but it's not (the two exceptions being semi-estranged from family and the spitting incident). Many of the locations mentioned exist in real life, although the farm and the people are all fictional, and the townsfolk of Elkton are much nicer and more welcoming than they are in Nicole's mind. There are several track records that were set in the late 1980s that have yet to be broken, however, which was a surprising discovery (calling all enterprising Elks looking to make history), Highway 38 does wash out quite a bit in very rainy winters, and the Umpqua River is a lot of fun to float (pro tip: be careful around the rapids by the high school).

All told, I wrote this hoping a part of myself that was lost would magically appear, when instead I should have been like Aubrey, actively seeking, connecting and driving over impossible gaps in the road. I can't say I'm there yet. But maybe I will be someday.

A question for the author

Q: What was your favorite children's book?

A: I was a very introverted, socially awkward child (this has not changed, although I am no longer a child), and I found my passion for reading very early. Since I read practically nonstop, this is both a tough and easy answer, but I have to say my favorite childhood book is *Matilda* by Roald Dahl.

The idea of a little girl sitting alone in a library surrounded by books and a bemused-but-rolling-with-it librarian appealed to me, along with the thought of that little girl being super incredibly smart and developing telepathic powers because of her unused brainpower. Of course, I am nothing like Matilda save for my love of books, and even there my tastes run towards genre fiction instead of the classics.

No book is entirely separate from the author, however, and I was heartbroken to realize Roald Dahl was a massive anti-Semite and all around deeply unpleasant person. That being said, Matilda holds a special place in my heart, while simultaneously the author can kick rocks...hopefully that is acceptable to say here.

About the author

Laurel Beckley is a writer, Marine Corps veteran, and librarian. She is from Eugene, Oregon, and currently lives in northern Virginia with her wife, fur creatures, and a collection of gently neglected houseplants.

thesuspectedbibliophile.home.blog, @laurelthereader

The Azurian Shield

Karl El-Koura

The day after he registered his daughter's birth, Bathar began conducting the inspections of the shield himself. Every morning, about an hour before dawn, he rode out through the villages that surrounded the castle, past the fields of farmland, through the forest, finally to the old woman's hut, to give her whatever he'd brought that morning. Then, riding his horse at the outer edge of the realm, he inspected the dome-shaped shield protecting them from the chaos without.

For seven months, that precaution proved unnecessary. The shield looked as it always had—a cloudy blue structure as solid as steel; it glowed brightly during the day and dimly at night. He could circumnavigate it in about an hour, making sure he detected none of the signs of deterioration that Ryon, the king's chief advisor and the last remaining mage in the realm, had taught him to look for. He saw nothing unusual, day after day of Alia's young life.

But, all of a sudden, that was no longer true. He'd ridden past a section on the northeast side, his glance dancing across the blue shield, when his mind registered something, and he pulled tight on the reins.

He dismounted and walked back, eyes fixed on the ground for now, willing what he'd seen—*thought he'd seen*—to be a trick of his mind.

Then he forced himself to look up.

A crack had begun to form on the shield. Like the shell of an egg that had been gently tapped, that still needed to be pulled apart.

Bathar stepped back. No one liked being this close to the shield; except for the tiny hut the exiled old woman had built for herself, the land at the edge of their realm was wild and uninhabited. The work of clearing out a perimeter around the shield, to ensure that no tree, shrub or weed obstructed the view of the guards charged with inspecting it, was reserved for the vilest criminals, and those hardened men and women would often have to be punished severely before they would carry out their task. Even the members of the royal guard—the best soldiers in the realm, his own command, whose duty it was to inspect the shield daily—had been visibly relieved when he'd announced he would henceforth conduct those inspections himself.

The shield had never bothered Bathar, though—just the opposite. As a young man, he'd *volunteered* to carry out the inspections. The shield kept them safe— why worry about anything beyond it? He felt comforted when he could see the cloudy blue steel and know that it continued to hold back the chaos.

But a cracking shield?

He took another step back, blinking furiously.

As he stared at the zigzag crack, starting at the bottom and reaching a few feet up the shield, all of the fears that kept others from traveling past the forest flooded into his mind. He imagined the crack growing, growing, bursting open with a wave of screeching monsters—hungry, frenzied creatures that had been deprived of human flesh for hundreds of generations. In his mind he saw a mass of fanged, upright bulls rush through the breach, their heavy footfalls shaking the ground, the shield collapsing around them in great chunks. The dark army rolled through him as if he weren't there, continued onto the realm he'd sworn to defend, killing the old woman, the farmers and the villagers, then those who lived within the castle walls. Cyna and Alia.

Alia.

In his fear, he'd forgotten—no, never that. For a moment he'd *neglected* to think what this meant for her...not the imagined army of his childhood nightmares, but the very real crack in the shield. By the oldest rules of the realm, as soon as a fissure was detected—the very morning—the youngest child would be brought to the site of the breach and sacrificed. That was the cost of the spell that would restore the shield. No child had yet been born since Alia.

He whistled for his horse, who came trotting over dutifully, blissfully unaware, even lifting her head and neighing in the direction of the crack, as if in disdain of the danger it hinted at.

The break in the shield hadn't expanded—not that Bathar had seen, anyway.

He grabbed the reins and swung himself on top of the horse, then urged her up the hill, back toward the castle. He had no definite plan as of yet, except that he didn't want any of his guard to know what he'd discovered until he was ready to tell them. And the king? Would he lie to the man he'd sworn to defend with his own life?

Yes—*his* life. Not Alia's; he'd never sworn that oath.

In his frantic race back, he almost rode through the old woman when she appeared in the middle of the worn path of trampled grass. She stood hunched over, her wispy hair like thin plumes of gray smoke in the dim early morning light, her short body covered in a patchwork of old clothes. He pulled up just in time to avoid trampling her over. She'd never moved.

He bit back the curse of frustration rising to his lips, then began to guide his horse around her.

"Wait," she said. Her voice, as usual, sounded like someone trying to speak while being choked.

Bathar ignored her, as he always did. Seventy years earlier, when the shield had last cracked, when the old woman was still young, and King Nebed newly installed on his throne, she had refused to perform the spell and sacrifice to seal the breach, insistent that no danger lay beyond. Her apprentice Ryon, a child himself at the time, had stepped forward and completed the ritual. The woman had been exiled to the shield as punishment, and a penalty of death placed on anyone who spoke to her.

In his childhood, Bathar's parents had told him stories of the Banished One, as a warning of what would happen to him if he didn't do as he was told. He'd always felt sorry for her, especially since she'd transgressed only because her mind had become sick. As a child, when he was beaten for his own small transgressions, he'd often wished that she would come to his aid. She had been the greatest mage the realm had seen for many generations, before her mind had turned against reality. Some rumors, then and now, whispered that the old woman retained her powers.

When he'd spotted her hut one morning while riding out of the forest, he'd resolved to do her a kindness in honor of his childhood sorrow at her plight—bring her something to eat, a few apples he'd gotten from the market the day before, or freshly baked bread he'd picked up that morning. He'd initially left them at the door of her hut, but in the last few months she'd been outside, waiting. Often she didn't even thank him with words, just bowed to him, her wrinkled face spreading into a faltering smile.

But she'd never before left her hut and come out as far as the makeshift road into the forest. Why on this morning, of all days?

He paused for a moment, to look her over and make sure she wasn't injured. It was hard to tell, with her. As soon as he'd met her, Bathar had understood why she'd never answered his childhood prayers for help. Would a woman with incredible powers choose to live a life of isolation and poverty in a wooden hut? Besides, she could barely speak in complete, calm sentences—should he believe she could cast spells? She seemed no worse than usual, though. He cleared his throat and indicated with a toss of his head that she should move out of the way.

"Bathar, please," she said.

He swallowed—he hadn't realized she knew his name.

"The shield doesn't protect us," she said. "No, no! It imprisons us. Is the king dying? Speak to Dara. There is no danger! You see? It wasn't cast to keep out chaos. No, no! In the time of the First King, yes? It was cast *over* us..."

Bathar stopped listening. Some days the old woman thanked him for his little morning gift with her crumbling smile, and he left quickly. Other days, awful days, she tried to make him stay by pretending to whisper dark secrets. But he didn't have time for tall tales of mythical kings on a regular day, let alone this one.

He nudged his horse past her as she continued to speak in her rushed, barely coherent way, as if the jumbled thoughts in her addled mind were all rushing out of her mouth at the same time and tripping over one another.

On the ride back, he pummeled the question of what could be done, furiously attacking it from every angle. But he was no further ahead by the time he rode through the castle's gatehouse. He handed his horse to the groom at the stables, grunting in response to the young man's friendly greeting. Normally he went straight into the keep after the morning inspections, but—this decision was clear at least—Cyna needed to be warned. He walked quickly across the central courtyard to their cottage, keeping his head low.

When he pushed open the wooden door, his wife said immediately, "You saw something?" She sat by the fire, nursing Alia.

He closed the door before nodding.

"How much time?" Cyna seemed to grip Alia tighter, as if she expected him to leap to her and rip their child out of her arms.

"I don't know," he said. "The crack wasn't there yesterday."

"They can't have her," she said.

"I know."

They looked down at the sleeping, feeding baby, the little face poking out of the blanket, the tiny fingers wrapped around Cyna's breast, the dimples in her knuckles.

"What are we going to do?" Cyna said, raising her own hand to brush back a wisp of hair from Alia's forehead.

Bathar didn't respond. Decisions had always come easily to him before. As a young royal guard, he'd had faith in the shield, which had protected them all his life. In the same way, he'd had faith in King Nebed, who had ruled over the realm since before Bathar was born. So when the king had executed a popular mayor who had criticized the royal family for their so-called acts of oppression, sparking a rebellion that swept up half the royal guard, Bathar had led the charge to subdue it. He'd never hesitated, never stopped to think whether the mayor was right or wrong—he'd sworn to defend king and realm, and he'd responded accordingly.

But now, for the first time in his life, he had no clarity of thought. This was a problem without solution.

Cyna's gray eyes studied his face. "We run away," she said.

"What?"

"The realm is a big place." They both knew it wasn't. His guard could search it in two days. "We hide, we keep moving."

He shook his head.

"Your old woman can help," she said. "Maybe she still has her powers. It wouldn't take much to hide us, would it?"

He'd never told Cyna that the old woman had spoken to him, or that on those occasions she'd seemed desperate to convince him that no danger existed beyond the shield, to infect him with her own madness. How could they trust their lives to her? "Suppose she can hide us," he said. "What happens when the shield falls?"

"We fight the monsters," she said immediately. "And if we die, we die fighting."

He shook his head again.

Cyna looked back at their child. "Then you have no other choice. It's time to... settle accounts."

Bathar stared at her, but she refused to meet his eyes. He'd saved King Nebed's life during the siege of the castle, so by law the king owed Bathar a life debt. But Bathar had been fulfilling a sworn oath. How could a debt accrue from someone carrying out their duty?

"Settle them how, Cyna? By sacrificing another child, even though our laws say it must be the youngest? All right—whom should the king slay instead?"

Tears began to form in her eyes, but she fought to hold them back.

"I'm sorry," he said, dropping to his knees. "I can't bear the thought of losing Alia." He wiped his wife's eyes gently. "But I also can't allow the shield to fall. I'm—"

A loud *rat-tat-tat* knock sounded at the door.

Cyna's glance dropped to the dagger he wore strapped to his thigh. He nodded, and she removed it, held it against her own thigh opposite the door.

Hand on the hilt of his sword, Bathar approached their entrance. He opened the door slowly.

One of his own soldiers stood outside, her gaze on the ground, kicking her boot into the dirt while she waited. She looked up as the door creaked open and said, "Are you alright, Sir?"

Bathar nodded curtly.

"The king would like to see you."

"About what?"

"Ryon didn't say. He bade me fetch you, and told me I'd find you at home. I thought maybe..."

"Everyone's fine," Bathar said. "I'll be there in a moment."

He closed the door, then walked back to his wife and child and kissed each one on the forehead.

"Give me time to find a solution," he said, withdrawing his sword. "But if anyone else comes through that door…"

He left the rest of the thought unspoken, then exchanged the sword for his dagger, and left without allowing himself a look back.

At the door to the keep, he heard from the guards that the king had taken a turn for the worse the previous night. King Nebed hadn't been able to make it to the throne room to conduct the day's business. Bathar rushed to the king's bedchamber, where the guards admitted him immediately.

Inside the curtains were drawn and the room dark, dimly lit by several candles. The king lay in bed under heavy covers, the princess Dara sitting on the large chair on the other side. Ryon had been pacing the floor but stopped when he saw Bathar.

"He's here, your majesty," he said.

"Bathar," the king said, the breath wheezing out of him. "Come close."

Bathar looked to Princess Dara for a sign of hope. She shook her head.

He kneeled beside the bed. "At your command, Majesty."

The king's eyes fluttered open. Even in the candlelight, his skin looked ashen, drained of blood and strength. His breath came in quick, shallow bursts. "This isn't easy for you, my son. But the realm must be protected at any cost. Dara will rule it well."

"Yes, your Majesty." For the moment, faced with this sight of infirmity from a man who for all of his life had been the symbol of power, he forgot about the shield. "But may your days be long still."

The king had closed his lips, but they came open again. A small smile played on the bloodless mouth. "You can see my days are finished." His words escaped in faint whispers interspersed with long pauses where he seemed to be gathering his strength. "But I die knowing that the sacrifice you make will preserve the kingdom for my daughter."

Bathar stood and faced the mage. "You know?"

Ryon had been listening from the end of the bed. "We know."

"How?"

"I saw the crack in the shield."

"But—if you're able to…what's the point of the inspections?"

"I could only see because you saw, Bathar."

A spying spell? Bathar hadn't thought that kind of power possible.

Without conscious thought, propelled by rage at this invasion of his mind, Bathar collapsed the distance between them. He towered over the shorter man, bent with age. Ryon's upturned gaze never left Bathar's. The cross scar, the intersecting diagonal slices like trenches dug into his face, always seemed deeper and redder when Ryon was struggling to restrain himself; Bathar had never seen them more pronounced.

Dara had risen from her seat and walked over, perhaps eager to diffuse the tension between the powerful mage and the chief royal guard.

She only put her hand on Bathar's shoulder, though.

Her presence—and the realization that knowledge of the shield's failure was no longer his own secret…and the corollary that Bathar had run out of time to plan an alternative that would save Alia's life— deflated his rising anger.

"Your Highness," he said, turning to face her. "I'm sorry I didn't—"

"I have no interest in dwelling on that," Dara said. "But we must move forward—and quickly."

Slaughter my daughter quickly, you mean. But what else was there to do? And what did she—or the dying king—or Ryon—care about Alia? She meant the world to him and to Cyna, but to them she was a child like any other in the realm. Except that this child had been marked out for an early, unnatural death. Her blood to him was precious, but to them it was simply currency, a price to be paid. To them the realm was the world, not one tiny creature.

So what else was there to do?

An answer appeared in his mind. Blood—or death? or suffering?—was required for the spell, but Cyna was right: it didn't have to be his daughter's.

As he'd been wading through those thoughts, the door had come open and two soldiers had stepped inside—not of his royal guard, strangely, but of the ranks who helped keep the peace in the realm. Bathar registered their presence without processing it. Dara and Ryon regarded him warily.

"Bathar," the king said.

Something about the old man's voice—even beyond how faded it sounded, as if the shadow of death had started to creep into it already—sent a cold shiver through Bathar's body.

He approached and bent down again.

"No one expects you to witness the sacrifice," the king said. "I have arranged quarters for you and Cyna in the keep. You can return to your cottage tonight."

Feeling that his body was a spring that had been compressed beyond endurance, Bathar willed it to keep still. He looked up at Ryon and Dara. On their candlelit, wary faces he saw all the confirmation he needed. He'd been called here as a pretense, to get him out of the way so that soldiers could be sent to his home to take Cyna and Alia captive.

He looked over his shoulder at the brutish soldiers. Likely two others stood outside the door, replacing his own guard, and more at the end of the hallway.

He had the dagger he wore strapped to his thigh, but he'd given Cyna his sword and hadn't thought to replace it before coming to see the king. With just that small weapon, could he fight his way past two?—four?—six soldiers on his own? Not to mention a mage who had the power, so it seemed, to invade his mind without his permission or even his awareness.

And even if he were successful somehow?

Despite his advanced age, Ryon had not yet chosen an apprentice, as he was supposed to do, as the old woman had done with him when she was yet very young. If Bathar killed Ryon now, and the old woman refused or was unable to make the sacrifice and cast the spell to seal the shield, then no one else could do it. Bathar would have sentenced *everyone* in the realm to a gruesome death.

Well—more realistically, the moment he reached for his dagger he'd be struck dead by Ryon, who continued to stare at him without blinking, who was perhaps even now reading his thoughts. And he'd have lost any chance of saving Alia. He would be dead, Alia would be sacrificed, and Cyna—what would happen to Cyna?

He filled his lungs with a deep breath and held it for a moment, then let it out and forced himself to nod. "I understand, Highness."

A dark, heavy, oppressive spirit seemed to leave the room at his words. He felt that even the soldiers by the door relaxed their stances.

"The shield must not fall," he continued, "and spilled blood is required to restore it. Your Highness, I offer my life in place of my daughter's."

The king opened his eyes. Some of the old man's strength seemed to come back into his voice. "Do you think you're the first father in our history who's offered to trade places with their child?"

"I—"

"The law is clear," Ryon said.

"If blood must be—"

"The law is not arbitrary. It must be the child born closest to the time the shield begins to fall."

"Why?" That question had never mattered before. It had been sufficient for Bathar to know that there was a mechanism to restore the shield should it begin to fail in his lifetime, and he hadn't stopped to give the details a second thought—until it was his own child at stake. They'd happily brought Alia to Ryon to register her, as required by law, on the first day after her birth. They'd seen it as a fun tradition, until it was done and they'd walked out into the courtyard that morning. Then he'd realized that the certificate of registration Ryon had signed for Alia could become her death sentence. Bathar had resolved to carry out the inspections of the shield himself. He vowed to begin doing so the very next day and to not stop…well, he hadn't allowed the thought to be explicit even in his own mind, let alone when speaking to Cyna about his plan…to not stop until the registry showed a new baby in the realm. But now that his worst fears had been realized—the reasonable fear that the shield might crack, and the secret fear that it would happen before another child was born—the question seemed so important that he wondered he'd never asked it before. That no one had asked those questions: why did the spell of restoration need a sacrifice at all? Why did it have to be the youngest child?

He stood and approached the mage. "Please, help me understand."

Ryon lowered his voice so the others couldn't hear. "That banished creature you see every morning—yes, I know about that too. She wanted to understand. She wanted to see beyond the shield. When her powers proved unequal to the task, she was willing to sacrifice the realm to satisfy her curiosity."

For a moment Bathar couldn't find his voice to defend himself. Then he whispered back, "I haven't broken his commandment. I've never said a single word to her. She's just a crazed, lonely, old woman."

And yet…in his youth, before he'd understood that the shield could be restored whenever it began to fail, he'd had nightmares in which he stood alone facing a cracking shield. The crack spread upward, like a tent being opened from the inside. The previous stillness shattered as the air filled with the sounds of netherworld creatures.

Where had those images come from? Cobbled together from stories told to scare him as a child.

More questions rushed into his thoughts, as if the first question—why did his daughter have to be sacrificed, when he was prepared to give up his own life?—had unlocked a secret door in his mind. The door had been holding back doubts and misgivings that it seemed had always been there, unseen.

The last time the shield had begun to crack, almost three-quarters of a century before, Ryon had restored it, as had the mage before him, and the one before. For how many generations?

Because since the days when the shield had been erected by powerful magic, it had never fallen—always restored in time, or the realm itself would have been destroyed. How long ago had that been? Even the number of generations was lost to time. In all of their recorded history—even in the legendary stories of the First King—the shield surrounded the realm as always.

What if the old woman had glimpsed a truth, mad as she was? What if the monsters beyond had died out in all of those generations; the chaos subdued in time? What if his ancestors had shut themselves in to survive a tempest, but the storm had passed—and they had no way of knowing?

"Was it wrong for the Banished to wonder what lay beyond the shield?" he said.

"Chaos," Ryon responded immediately.

"Chaos once—but chaos now?"

"Chaos always."

Not good enough, Bathar thought, but didn't say. Not if it meant his child's life. He sensed more than saw the soldiers move closer to him.

He returned to the bed and knelt beside the prone king again, but spoke in normal tones rather than the reverential whisper he'd been using. "Highness—how do we know the danger persists? Let me report on what lies beyond. If I don't return within a set time, Ryon will be ready to seal the shield."

"And what comes through during your set time, Bathar?" the king said.

"My guard is ready to defend the realm." He'd promised Cyna he would think of something, and now he had. It would give them a chance. "At the first sign of trouble, you can—"

"No," Princess Dara said.

He turned to her sharply. "But—"

She raised an eyebrow.

"Highness?" he said to Nebed in frustrated desperation, then immediately recognized the mistake he'd made in appealing to the dying king over Dara.

"You are too valuable to the realm, Bathar," she said.

"Princess, I—"

"She has spoken, Bathar," the king said. "Do not test our patience further."

Frustration and desperation had pushed him into insulting the princess, and now a new wellspring of those feelings propelled him even further. "You are still the monarch," he said, standing and looking down at the king. "And you will grant me this request."

"Watch yourself—"

"I demand repayment."

The dark spirit that had departed only minutes before returned with renewed vigor, filling the air and making it heavy. The sudden invasion of that spirit also stole whatever response the king had been preparing to make. He shut his mouth, but his yellowed eyes filled with disgust.

After he'd saved his life, the king had demanded that Bathar ask him anything —up to half the realm's riches, he'd said. Bathar had refused reward for doing his duty. Now he understood why the king had been so adamant: he'd wanted the debt paid, at a price he'd set himself. The king had relented only reluctantly— perhaps, if it were true that Ryon could invade minds, after consulting with his advisor. Ryon might have reassured him that Bathar would never call in the debt.

Well, Ryon had been wrong. The thought comforted Bathar.

"My life is almost at an end," the king said, "and isn't worth what it once was. You, however, Bathar, are valuable. You will defend my daughter when she ascends to the throne, if she'll still have you. And you will help defend the realm at the shield's breach until we restore it."

Bathar didn't understand—the king seemed to be saying yes and no at the same time. He waited for the slow words to emerge.

"If you can convince her to accept, I will allow your wife to go through the breach. If she refuses, however, the debt is repaid."

The thin lips twisted into a sneer as the king watched the changes that must have been visible on Bathar's face. He didn't believe the stated reason—no one man was so valuable to the defense of the realm. No, this was the king's cruelty asserting itself—the cruelty that had sparked the rebellion that Bathar himself had helped quell. Even as he lay dying, Nebed had found a way to lash out at him.

"You're both young," the king said, interrupting his thoughts. "You can have another child."

How had he served such a mind of cold calculations? But he knew: it was easy to justify the king's severity as necessary when the decisions didn't directly affect him, easier to support the throne he'd sworn allegiance to than question the morality of its actions.

Bathar sighed deeply, then stood. "Can I see my family?" he said.

The two soldiers stepped forward at a sign from the king, and he gave the order. Bathar left without looking back. Two more soldiers stood outside the door as he'd guessed, and two more at either end of the hall. He was led across the staircase to the east wing of the castle, then down more hallways until they reached another door, similarly guarded by a pair of soldiers. They stepped aside to allow Bathar to enter.

Inside, Cyna paced the large room, while Alia slept curled up in the middle of the bed. Cyna turned a ferocious look on him when he opened the door, which resolved into joy. But the hopeful smile started decaying almost immediately.

"What happened?" she said as he said to her, "Are you all right?" Her right arm had been bandaged, and a pool of blood had leaked through to stain the white wrapping.

They sat on the edge of the bed and spoke in hushed tones out of a habit of not wanting to wake Alia. Cyna told him about fighting the soldiers who had come to their home, and how she'd eventually had to surrender to them. Bathar told her about his suspicion that the chaos beyond the shield might have resolved into order through the intervening generations, and how he had used his life debt to—

Cyna grabbed his leg. "You asked him to let you through the shield?"

"Yes."

She stared at him. He knew from the way her jaw clenched that she was imagining him dying a thousand ugly deaths.

"He won't let me go through, Cyna. He said he would allow *you* to. He's hoping that you won't."

She looked back at the tiny figure sleeping soundly in the large bed. "You were willing," she said softly.

"Willing, but terrified. We can figure out another way."

The door came open and Ryon strode in.

"Well?" he said, as they stood to face him. "Will she go?"

Bathar looked at Cyna.

"Yes," she said.

"Fine," Ryon said, then tossed a disdainful sneer at Bathar. "The king has allowed this concession as payment in full for a debt no subject should hold over his sovereign."

"I'd like some time to—" Bathar began.

"The crack has started to spread. We ride out immediately." He faced Cyna. "My assistants are already carrying out the stone of sacrifice. We'll overtake them, and you'll have until they reach the shield to leave our realm...if you can go through with it...and return...if you do return."

"How do you know it's started to spread?" But in asking the question, Bathar realized the most probable explanation—Ryon had not cast a spell that could invade the mind of an unwilling subject: he'd commissioned a spy to follow Bathar on his inspections. That spy had opened his mind to Ryon and allowed him to see the crack that morning; and he saw it now, spreading.

Ryon's disdainful sneer turned into an amused smile, and then a puff of air escaped his mouth, as if that were the only response Bathar deserved. Cyna had gone around the bed and picked up Alia, cradling her to keep from waking her.

"She rides with me," Ryon said, extending his arms.

Cyna and Bathar exchanged glances.

"That creature will save our kingdom," Ryon said. "No harm will come to her before we reach the shield, believe me."

After another moment of hesitation, Cyna placed Alia in Ryon's arms.

In the central courtyard a retinue of twenty-four regular soldiers waited on twenty-four horses. Attendants brought the princess and Ryon their own steeds.

"My guard can best defend against whatever comes through the shield," Bathar said, looking up at Ryon.

The old man shook his head. "They are needed here. We cannot delay—here come your horses, and swords for you and Cyna, in case a sword can even help her on the other side. You take the front."

They rode in silence. A line of a dozen soldiers separated Bathar and Cyna from their daughter; Ryon rode beside Princess Dara, and the remaining soldiers drew up the rear. After twenty minutes, they overtook the caravan transporting the sacrificial altar, a pair of mules pulling the wagon on which the concave table had been placed. It looked like an oversized creche with ornate golden legs.

Bathar resisted the temptation to stare at it as they rode past.

When they arrived within sight of the shield, Bathar drew in his breath. The zigzag crack had opened up at the bottom where it met the earth, so that a hole the size of a coin had appeared between their world and whatever lay beyond.

By the time he and Cyna had ridden down the grassy hill to stand a few feet from the shield, the hole had grown even more, now large enough to admit a small mouse. And yet—nothing came through. Or did it? He found it uncomfortable to keep his eyes fixed on that hole. As if a blinding power were seeping through already, burning the eyes of any who dared gaze upon it.

If simply *looking* at the light coming through could cause pain, what would happen to Cyna when she stepped into that world?

He turned his horse to face his wife, whose gaze was fixed on the shield. "Cyna —" he began, but she shook her head slightly.

A crowd started gathering on the hill, villagers and farmers tempted by the royal procession to follow and see what the commotion was about.

Perhaps righteously—or perhaps desperately seeking a distraction—Bathar felt anger rising up toward them. Would he allow their presence to turn his daughter's sacrifice into a performance? Did Cyna have to go through the shield with gawkers watching her every step? And what if her courage failed her?

He brought his horse around and approached Princess Dara, standing with Ryon at the foot of the hill, waiting for the caravan. The soldiers closed in against him.

The princess called out to let him through.

"I beg permission to disperse the crowd," he said to her. "I don't want spectators."

She shrugged, then nodded.

He turned and galloped his horse up the hill toward the largest part of the crowd, then suddenly pulled up on the reins. Covered in a patchwork of frayed and faded clothes, bent over, trying to hide behind others—his glance picked her out. The old woman.

He dismounted and followed her as she tried to disappear among the others.

"You shouldn't be here," he whispered, grabbing her and pulling her away from the pocket of people.

The hunched over head covered in a tattered shawl looked up at him as her smaller legs tried to keep up. "You...speak to me?"

He looked around to make sure no one was watching. "I'm sorry I never did before. You say there's no danger beyond the shield. Do you have any evidence?"

"Evidence?" She laughed, an ugly, croaking sound. "Destroyed! All destroyed!"

Bathar hissed to keep quieter. "What was destroyed?"

"Old—very old—*forbidden* texts. Buried, you see? I discovered them—I recovered them! Gone now...destroyed— guess by whom?—but I have them in my head." She tapped a finger against her skull. She spoke quickly now, eagerly, as if a bottle had been unstopped and all the words began spilling out like wine. "We did not cast the shield. Six other kingdoms cast it *over* us. To protect themselves from *us*, you understand? We caused great suffering in those days, and our cruel king vowed to never rest until he ruled all of the realms. So their greatest mages united to imprison us in the shield. It would fall once the king died and was replaced by a new monarch—as long as that one renounced cruelty." She began to cackle. "It didn't have the intended effect! When he saw his mages were powerless to destroy the shield, the king buried the truth. He insisted that the shield protected his realm, destroyed all of our previous records, and began to call himself the 'First King'!" She cackled again.

"Be quiet!" Bathar barked, keeping her moving. "How certain are you that those things are true?"

"My life." She spoke quietly now, deflated again. "I gave up my life."

Did he believe her? He wanted to, more than anything.

"Then sacrificing the youngest child is not required to seal the shield?" he said.

"No, and neither is the so-called spell. Any cruel act under the authority of the new ruler would suffice. You see? Our laws *are* arbitrary."

Bathar continued to stare at her. Her mind didn't seem as addled as he'd once thought. "You said you discovered old texts?"

"Protected scrolls. Buried in jars, secretly in the time of the First King, in the deepest part of the forest behind the castle. I sensed their magic—not a mage in a dozen could've found them. But I could. I did! Not a mage in a hundred could've opened the jars, you understand?"

Bathar nodded for her to go on. She seemed like a child desperately seeking approval.

"My mistake—I brought the truth to Nebed, prince of the realm then, because I believed he would be more reasonable than his mad father. Nebed destroyed the scrolls."

"Why?"

"Fear!" she yelled. "Generations of it, deep in our blood. He said the scrolls were a hoax by someone—he implied me!—who wanted to see the realm destroyed. Instead he had the *scrolls* destroyed, forbade me or anyone from speaking of them again. It didn't matter at first, but soon the mad king died and Nebed ascended to the throne, and the shield began to crack...and I begged for permission to allow us a glimpse—to prove the truth—"

"He refused, and he exiled you."

The old woman shook her head, smiled impishly. "He tried to have me killed. The scoundrel Ryon wasn't born with that double scar! I exiled myself, to watch over the shield. I've been waiting for this day ever since."

Bathar stopped looking around furtively and focused all of his attention on the old woman. He held her face in his hands, to stare into her eyes. "Then there is no danger beyond the shield? You're sure?"

She leaned her face against the warmth of his skin. He suddenly remembered that she hadn't felt human touch for seven decades. "No more than inside the shield," she said, her voice now soft and calm. "Less."

"Then why does it hurt to look at it?"

The gummy, toothless mouth opened in a smile. She looked past him at the shield. "I wanted to live long enough for a glimpse of that world." She stared at it for a while as he continued to study her face, still trying to decide if she was crazy or telling the truth, and if he could risk Cyna's life on his assessment. "It hurts your eyes, young man," she said, "because the light is brighter there. We have grown accustomed to darkness."

A murmur from those around him made him look over his shoulder, back down at the shield. The hole had grown significantly; if a mouse could've squeezed through before, now something the size of a large cat would have been able to dart into their world.

He told the old woman to stay hidden in the crowd, then whistled for his horse. Bathar rode down to Ryon; the soldiers seemed to accept now that he didn't intend harm and allowed him to approach.

Alia began to cry for him, and reflexively Bathar reached out for her, but Ryon shook his head.

"Why does nothing come through the hole?" Bathar said. "If chaos reigns beyond, why isn't it spilling into our world already?"

The satisfaction on Ryon's face made him realize how desperate he must have sounded. "You do not have to sacrifice your wife to the darkness."

"I just want to understand."

A horn sounded, announcing the arrival of the caravan and ordering the crowds to make way for it. As Bathar watched, the mules crested the hill.

"Once the stone is set up," Ryon said, "the ritual will be completed."

"No," Bathar said. "The king—"

Dara spoke up. "We can't risk the realm." She motioned toward the hole, which had grown even more, but still not enough to admit Cyna. "It is in the hands of the gods."

Bathar's horse turned one way and then the other, working out Bathar's own nervous energy. None of his royal guard had been allowed to accompany them, although his guard could best hold back whatever chaos spilled out. And to do what? Protect the dying king? No, Ryon and Dara had never intended to allow Cyna to leave.

Sensing trouble, the soldiers closed in around Ryon and the princess.

He took a deep breath and guided his horse back toward Cyna, who stood staring at the growing crack in the shield.

"They won't wait," he said. "Once the stone is in place, they're going to sacrifice Alia."

Cyna looked up at him. Something had changed in her. She'd been staring resolutely at the hole, the painful bright light Ryon called darkness, and in her unblinking eyes he saw none of the things he expected—no trepidation, no fear, no anxiety. Only resolution. Not a muscle moved on her face as she looked at him— looked *through* him, he felt.

Now that the caravan had arrived, the soldiers dismounted their horses and, with Princess Dara and Ryon at their center, began moving closer to the crack in the shield, to prepare for the sacrifice.

Cyna watched them pass by silently, then she leapt onto her horse and rode out toward the foothill, yelling: "By leave of our king, ruler of this realm, I have been granted permission to cross that threshold!"

Bathar followed, and soon he understood what she was doing. The crowd had begun to approach to hear the message Cyna was shouting as she rode back and forth. A panicked murmur went through them. They'd come out of curiosity, which had turned to fear as they saw the crack in the shield, but the soldiers had reassured them. Now they were waiting to see a once in a lifetime event, the sealing of the shield. But one of their own people *choosing* to cross over wasn't a lifetime event—it had never happened in the history of their realm. The anxious, pressing people slowed the descent of the caravan, so that the horn had to be blown repeatedly.

"Can't you see with your own eyes?" Cyna now yelled. "There is no danger!"

She repeated the words like a mantra. Then, finally turning her horse around, she called out: "Come and see!"

The crowd was thrown into confusion. Some people—more than Bathar would have imagined—began to pull away from the others, to follow Cyna, approach the breach, see for themselves. Another group seemed to be chasing the first to pull them back. The better part of the crowd retreated a little further up the hill, perhaps afraid the approach of their fellows would finally cause whatever was waiting on the other side to come pouring through. Bathar looked for the old woman, found her being jostled by the waves of people as she tried to push forward. He rode toward her, then dismounted and helped her onto his horse, where she'd be safe from being trampled to death.

"She's going through the shield?" the old woman said, excitedly, reverentially.

The caravan was almost down the hill.

He swung himself back onto the horse, grabbing the reins around the old woman to keep her steady, and galloped forward, cutting through the smaller crowd.

A line of a dozen soldiers stood in front of the breach, masking it. But they faced inwards, their backs to the shield. Just in front of them the remaining guards formed a circle around Ryon, still holding Alia protectively, and Princess Dara.

Cyna was on her feet and trying to press through, but two soldiers had stepped forward to hold her back.

Bathar rode up beside her horse and handed the reins to the old woman as he dismounted. The smaller crowd was filling in the space behind them. The caravan's horn sounded again, more angrily; it was almost on top of them.

He approached the soldiers, two more stepping forward to meet him.

Behind him, more than thirty or forty of the villagers and farmers had gathered. They were young, strong, brave—but wary. They tried to look past the soldiers at the breach, as big as a large dog now, and murmured among themselves. He felt that curiosity and excitement had brought them this far—with two dozen armed men and women still between them and the shield—but that they were on the verge of retreating to join the others on the hill.

But if Cyna—and he!—proved that no danger existed? Would they follow?

In a loud voice, he yelled: "You will honor our king and his wishes! You will allow us to cross to the other side!"

Ryon turned his head to Dara and whispered in her ear. The princess touched the shoulder of the soldier in front of her, who moved out of the way. She stepped forward and said, just as loudly, "You dare speak of honor, you who have broken my father's law?" Her glance jumped to the bundle of rags gathered on his saddle, and a spasm of displeasure seized her features. Then, in a lower voice: "Your debt is repaid; you will not be killed for this disobedience, though you will live like her as a banished one."

"Highness—don't you want to know what lies beyond?"

Her glance now jumped to Cyna. "What will a mother not say to save her child? There is nothing beyond the shield but chaos. She would save one child and bring ruin to our kingdom."

The horn sounded right behind them, and Bathar turned desperately to see the smaller crowd parting to admit the mules carrying the stone table.

He grabbed Cyna by the arm and led her back to their horses. "They won't believe you even if you go," he said.

"They'll say it's a trick, a lie. You were corrupted by the darkness. It won't matter."

She looked over her shoulder. "Then we fight."

We're outnumbered, he thought but didn't say. *They'll kill us.*

The heavy stone altar with its large curving legs had been placed on the ground. Ryon set Alia down in the middle of that cold, dead table. Over the neighing of the anxious horses and the rumbling nervousness of the crowd, Bathar could hear his daughter's unhappy cries.

Ryon lifted up a long golden dagger, then his voice bellowed out, deeper and stronger than Bathar had ever heard it, speaking the words of incantation, at the end of which he'd plunge the knife into the tiny body.

One moment Bathar had been despairing, certain they'd run out of options. The next, he knew only that his daughter wanted to be picked up, and that nothing more than a circle of soldiers and the possibility of death stood in his way.

He unsheathed his sword. Without a word, Cyna did the same.

They fought desperately, Bathar keeping one ear on Ryon's voice, unsure how long the incantation would last. Finally, they were almost at the stone table, and with a cry from deep within his belly, Bathar descended on the next soldier, the only one—for the moment—standing between him and Ryon. The soldier fell backward, his head cracking against one of the golden legs.

Ryon stopped speaking and his cold stare dropped to meet Bathar's. With one arm Bathar leveled his sword at him, while he reached out for Alia with the other, his gaze never leaving Ryon's.

The old mage smiled, then flicked his head to one side. As if obeying a wordless command, the sword flew out of Bathar's hand.

Before he could register what had happened, Bathar saw Ryon plunge the dagger through the air. Bathar leapt forward—or tried to—to stop or deflect or absorb the thrust. But his body didn't react. Ryon had immobilized him and now he would stand, helpless, and watch his daughter be killed.

Except, the dagger had stopped just above her bundled, wriggling, crying body, the sharp golden weapon shaking in

Ryon's hands as if caught between two unseen but powerful and opposing forces.

Bathar felt the tightness in his body release. He stumbled forward and snatched his daughter from the table, held her close to his body. Then he allowed himself to look around.

Four panicked soldiers surrounded Princess Dara protectively, leading her back toward the shield—even toward the breach. The rest of her contingent was engaged in battle—because it wasn't only Cyna who fought them. Had those farmers and villagers joined the fight, he wondered, because they finally accepted that no danger lay beyond? Or, as he suspected most likely, because they saw this as an opportunity to defy, maybe even punish, the daughter of a cruel and oppressive king?

Out of the corner of his eye he became aware of a hunched-over pile of rags, a single arm sticking out from the sleeve, the fingers of its shaking hand outstretched. He turned his head as the old woman collapsed, then Bathar heard a loud clang as the dagger stabbed the stone table with all of Ryon's previously restrained force.

In the next moment, a mournful, drawn-out sound filled the skies, an amplified call from the magically enhanced longhorn set on the roof of the castle keep. The king had died.

Bathar leapt forward and grabbed the knife from the ground where it had tumbled, expecting a struggle with Ryon—but he couldn't see the mage anywhere. He spun on his heels and ran to help the old woman to her feet.

She pushed his hand away weakly. "Go," she said, her voice faint. "Go through the shield."

He moved his arm around hers and grabbed her, helped her to her feet. She felt as insubstantial as a bale of hay. "Come with us."

"Do you see?" she said, looking past him, her wrinkled face radiant. "I told you."

He followed her gaze. The hole had grown, as large as the giant door to the throne room, and seemed to be expanding even as he watched. Beyond it lay another world, a bright world, an expanse of green grass and large trees. Something was invading through the breach in the shield indeed, but it was light; like casting aside a thick curtain in a dark room. The world beyond was almost too bright to look at.

"Please come with us," he said.

Her hand dropped to touch the side of Alia's face, who giggled in response. She looked back at Bathar and—almost reluctantly—allowed herself to nod, relief making her face relax into a toothless smile. She'd been ostracized for so long, he understood, that even this small display of kindness seemed to touch her deeply.

Bathar whistled for his horse. But before the animal could reach them, he felt someone tugging at Alia, trying to rip her out of his arm. He turned quickly but no one was near him except the old woman.

"Go," she said, and seemed to gather up her remaining energy. The relief on her face had been replaced by exhaustion. But she raised her arm, and immediately Bathar felt the force release its grip on his daughter.

"Go," she said again, straining to speak. "I'll follow."

Bathar climbed atop the horse, holding Alia close.

The old woman's arm was shaking, but he couldn't see Ryon—not near the stone table on golden legs; not near the hole in the shield, where Cyna and her small upstart army of villagers and farmers had chased the princess and her remaining guards; and not on the hill, where the rest of the crowd watched and waited to see what would happen.

He galloped his horse forward, toward the fighting. "Stop!" he cried. "The shield is falling!"

Like an incantation of his own, the words seemed to wake them up to that reality, especially the princess—queen, now—and her soldiers, who had been so focused on defending themselves that they'd retreated toward the breach.

With a loud command from their queen, the soldiers took a step back, toward the shield. Cyna issued her own command and her fighters fell back too. Bathar led his horse in between the two forces.

"My queen," he said. "Look and see—there is nothing to fear. Lead your people!"

The queen pushed aside one of her soldiers and stepped forward. She looked past Bathar and addressed Cyna's small army: "Troops to outnumber you ten to one will be here shortly. They will crush

you without mercy unless you lay down
your arms.”

"The shield will fall, Highness," Bathar
said.

"As for you," she said, as if he hadn't
spoken, "surrender now and I promise you
and your wife a painless execution."

"Please—you can lead us to the other
side."

From the set expression on her face,
though, he knew she never would;
because underneath that forced
expression, he detected terror. What could
convince her that the image beyond the
breach wasn't an illusion? Would she
believe even if someone crossed over and
returned?

She looked past him again, and a smile
stretched out her thin lips. The
reinforcements had arrived—he knew it
even as he turned his head to see the line
of horses crest the hill.

Bathar looked at Cyna, then to the
others. "There is nothing to fear!" he
yelled.

The queen's soldiers had closed in
around her and began to move her away
from the shield. Bathar reached down for
Cyna, pulled her onto the back of his

horse, then galloped ahead and through the large, arch-like breach.

Squinting at the unnatural brightness, he took a deep breath; the air felt as fresh as any morning he'd ever experienced.

He turned his horse and waited to see if anyone else would cross. But already a few were coming through—slowly, hesitantly, then turning and calling and waving to others to follow.

"I have to help the old woman," Bathar said to his wife.

Cyna nodded, dismounted, eagerly accepted Alia from him.

"Be careful," she said. Then her expression softened and she put her free hand on his knee. "Bathar," she said, with a new voice, "we're outside the shield."

Bringing up an arm to protect his eyes, he allowed himself a look around at the verdant field stretching out endlessly before him, forests of tall, majestic trees to each side. Another blue shield surrounded them, rising up from the horizon, a giant and distant sky, like the reality on which their pale imitation had been based.

He looked back at his wife and returned her beaming smile.

Through the breach in the shield, which had grown as large as the castle gatehouse, he saw that the queen had retreated to the foothill, her tiny regiment reunited with the reinforcements. Incredibly, they were organizing themselves into defensive lines. Queen Dara still expected monstrous hordes to come pouring through.

A small group of soldiers, led by Ryon, were marching toward him. One of them carried the old woman over his shoulder like a bag of flour.

For a brief moment, Bathar's confused gaze met Ryon's. Ryon lifted an arm and the golden dagger, which Bathar had shoved into his tunic, began to shake.

"No!" he yelled, and tried to grab it. The blade sliced across his palm as it flew through the air, then the hilt landed in Ryon's waiting hand.

Now Bathar understood: they weren't marching toward the breach, but to the stone table. They were bringing the woman there to sacrifice her; despite what was written in the law, Ryon had convinced the queen that the death of the old woman would suffice to seal the breach.

Desperately, Bathar tried to nudge his horse forward, but his arms and legs didn't respond. He'd been immobilized again. To watch the old woman die and do nothing?

It's not Ryon holding you back.

The voice inside his head reminded him of the old woman's, but full of strength and vigor.

He ignored it and willed his body to respond.

Ryon does not have the power to speak directly into anyone's mind. I will release you if you promise to stay where you are.

They dropped her on top of the stone table. Ryon stood over her, the golden dagger lifted high, his mouth moving with the words of incantation.

I can help you! Bathar screamed at her in his mind, then realized what he was saying. *If you have this kind of power, can't you stop them?*

To what end? My mind is strong, but my body is spent. I prayed to live long enough to see beyond the shield. I never imagined that I'd see any of our people cross to the other side. Or that I'd be able to send a piece of myself with you. Now, enough about that. Isn't this something? Ryon, petulant child that he was, claimed he didn't believe a word of what I said about the shield or our laws. But you see? Some part of him believes.

You don't have to— Bathar began, but the thought died out as Ryon brought down his arm, plunging the dagger into the old woman. A blink, and then Bathar saw nothing but cloudy blue steel.

Bathar dropped from his horse, then fell to his knees, staring at the shield.

After a few moments, he felt a hand on his back. Cyna, holding their baby.

"Look," she said, laughing.

Alia seemed to be playing a game, lifting her mother's necklace and letting it drop—except that her hands never moved, only her eyes.

"She said that a piece of her would come with us." Bathar ran his fingers against the side of the tiny, soft face. "Hello, little mage. Maybe one day you can help us show the truth to everyone trapped inside."

In response Alia giggled, her brown eyes shining.

Bathar kissed her forehead, then hugged them both tightly. After a while, he said, "We're falling behind."

Riding together on Bathar's horse, they followed the small crowd of freed people to discover the world that lay beyond.

See Karl El-Koura's story "The Azurian Shield" online at Metaphorosis.
If you liked it, leave a comment. Authors love that!
Remember to subscribe to our e-mail updates so you'll know when new stories are posted.

About the story

Some time ago, an image popped into my head of a soldier on a horse in a field, facing a cracking dome from the inside. I was so excited by the idea that I started writing the story almost right away (often, though not always, a mistake). I wrote about a thousand words of the soldier trying to hold the line while monstrous creatures poured through. I had this notion that the magic of the shield could only protect them while a righteous king or queen sat on the throne, but after about a thousand words the idea ran out of steam.

From time to time, I thought about that poor soldier facing the cracking shield, but I didn't have a strong sense of where to take the story.

Then one day it occurred to me: what if the shield isn't there to keep chaos out? What if they only thought it did? And what if the price to keep the shield whole is a terrible one?

I began to see the outline of this new version of the story: my soldier, named Bathar now, and head of the elite guard sworn to defend the realm, would have a deep need to ensure that the shield didn't fall (which would lead, as he supposed, to the destruction of the kingdom). But he'd also be unable to pay the terrible price required to restore a failing shield. An impossible position--except for the possibility of recovering a forgotten truth about their situation. That line of thinking seemed to unlock the story for me. Now when I started writing, I didn't stop until I had a fair-sized novelette.

A question for the author

Q: What five words describe you?

A: I can't distill the essence of my being into five words! I'd need six, maybe even seven.

That aside, one of the interesting things I've noticed is how much more joy I get from making a little bit of money from selling one of my stories compared with making much more money doing anything else. I sold my first story in 1997 for $15, and I carried the check (yes, paper check in those days) and danced around the house.

I'm less demonstrative these days, but the joy at selling something I've written remains in many ways undiminished. Why, when the reward is so minuscule, especially compared to the effort involved? I think it's the idea that you're being recognized—materially, tangibly—for something you love doing, and that you'd carry on doing even if no one paid any attention. But it is nice when someone pays attention, when an editor looks at something you've written and says, "That's pretty good. I'll pay to publish that."

So the five words I'm choosing to describe myself: "Writes; writes for money, happily."

About the author

Karl El-Koura lives with his family in Canada's capital city. He holds a second-degree black belt in Okinawan Goju Ryu karate, is an avid commuter-cyclist (on a stationary bike, lately), and works for the Canadian Federal Public Service.

www.ootersplace.com, @KarlElKoura

Copyright

Title information

Metaphorosis October 2021

ISSN: 2573-136X (online)
ISBN: 978-1-64076-209-1 (e-book)
ISBN: 978-1-64076-210-7 (paperback)

Copyright

Metaphorosis Magazine is an imprint of
Metaphorosis Publishing
Neskowin, OR, USA

www.metaphorosis.com

Discounts available

Substantial discounts are available for educational institutions, including writing workshops. Discounts are also available for quantity purchases. For details, contact Metaphorosis at metaphorosis.com/about

Metaphorosis Publishing

Metaphorosis offers beautifully written science fiction and fantasy. Our imprints include:

Metaphorosis Magazine
Plant Based Press
Verdage

You can also find us:
@MetaphorosisMag, @MetaphorosisRev, @Metaphorosis
www.facebook.com/metaphorosis

Help keep Metaphorosis running by supporting us at
Patreon.com/metaphorosis

See more about some of our books on the following pages.

Metaphorosis
a magazine of speculative fiction

Metaphorosis is an online speculative fiction magazine dedicated to quality writing. We publish an original story every week, along with author bios, interviews, and notes on story origins.

We also publish monthly print and e-book issues, as well as yearly Best of and Complete anthologies.

Come and see us online at magazine.Metaphorosis.com

Metaphorosis:
Best of 2020

The best science fiction and fantasy stories from *Metaphorosis* magazine's fifth year.

Metaphorosis
2020

All the stories from *Metaphorosis* magazine's fifth year. Fifty-two great SFF stories.

Metaphorosis: Best of 2019

The best science fiction and fantasy stories from *Metaphorosis* magazine's fourth year.

Metaphorosis 2019

All the stories from *Metaphorosis* magazine's fourth year. Fifty-two great SFF stories.

Metaphorosis:
Best of 2018

The best science fiction and fantasy stories from *Metaphorosis* magazine's third year.

Metaphorosis
2018

All the stories from *Metaphorosis* magazine's third year. Fifty-two great SFF stories.

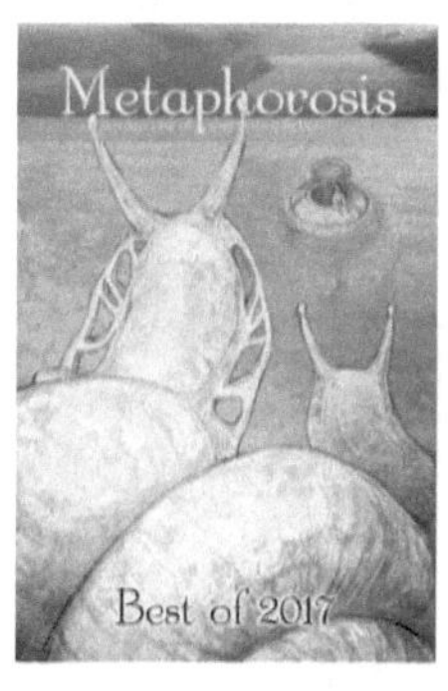

Metaphorosis: Best of 2017

The best science fiction and fantasy stories from *Metaphorosis* magazine's *second* year.

Metaphorosis 2017

All the stories from *Metaphorosis* magazine's second year. Fifty-three great SFF stories.

Metaphorosis:
Best of 2016

The best science fiction and fantasy stories from *Metaphorosis* magazine's first year.

Metaphorosis
2016

Almost all the stories from *Metaphorosis* magazine's first year.

Plant Based Press

Vegan-friendly science fiction and fantasy, including an annual anthology of the year's best SFF stories.

Best Vegan SFF of 2020

The best vegan-friendly science fiction and fantasy stories of 2020!

Best Vegan SFF of 2019

The best vegan-friendly science fiction and fantasy stories of 2019!

Best Vegan SFF
of 2018

The best vegan-friendly science fiction and fantasy stories of 2018!

Best Vegan SFF
of 2017

The best vegan-friendly science fiction and fantasy stories of 2017!

Best Vegan SFF
of 2016

The best vegan-friendly science fiction and fantasy stories of 2016!

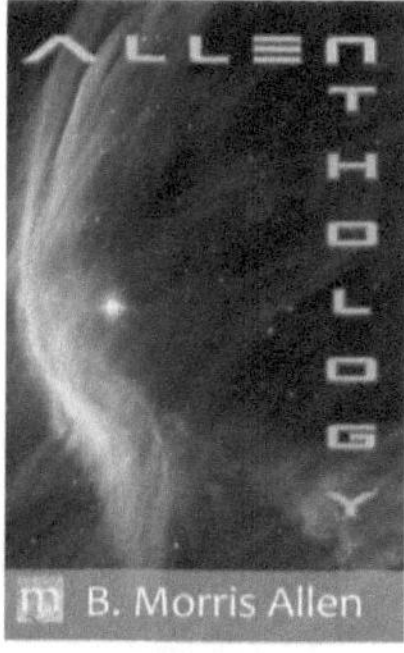

Susurrus

A darkly romantic story of magic, love, and suffering.

Allenthology: Volume I

A quarter century of SFF, including the full contents of the collections *Tocsin, Start with Stones,* and *Metaphorosis.*

Verdage

Verdage

Science fiction and fantasy books for writers – full of great stories, often with an additional focus on the craft of speculative fiction writing.

Reading 5X5 x2

Duets

How do authors' voices change when they collaborate?

A round-robin of five talented science fiction and fantasy authors collaborating with each other and writing solo.

Including stories by Evan Marcroft, David Gallay, J. Tynan Burke, L'Erin Ogle, and Douglas Anstruther.

Score

an SFF symphony

What if stories were written like music? *Score* is an anthology of varied stories arranged to follow an emotional score from the heights of joy to the depths of despair – but always with a little hope shining through.

Reading 5X5

Five stories, five times

Twenty-five SFF authors, five base stories, five versions of each – see how different writers take on the same material.

Reading 5X5

Writers' Edition

Two extra stories, the story seed, and authors' notes on writing. Over 100 pages of additional material specifically aimed at writers.

Vestige

Novelettes, novellas, and novels by Metaphorosis authors.